OPAL
MOONBABY
and the OUT OF
THIS WORLD ADVENTURE

Have you read all of the *Opal Moonbaby* books?

- ☐ Opal Moonbaby and the Best Friend Project
- ☑ Opal Moonbaby and the Out of this World Adventure
- ☐ Opal Moonbaby and the Summer Secret

OPAL

MOONBABY

and the OUT OF
THIS WORLD ADVENTURE

Maudie Smith

Cover illustration by Tony Ross
Inside illustrations by Dave Shepherd

Orion
Children's Books

First published as *About Zooming Time, Opal Moonbaby!*
in Great Britain in 2013
by Orion Children's Books
This new edition published in 2015
by Orion Children's Books
an imprint of Hachette Children's Group
a division of Hodder and Stoughton Ltd
Orion House
5 Upper St Martin's Lane
London WC2H 9EA
A Hachette UK Company

1 3 5 7 9 10 8 6 4 2

A catalogue record for this book is available from the British Library.

ISBN 978 1 4440 1582 9

Printed and bound in Great Britain by Clays Ltd, St Ives plc

The paper and board used in this paperback are natural and recyclable
products made from wood grown in sustainable forests. The manufacturing
processes conform to the environmental regulations of the country of origin.

www.orionchildrensbooks.co.uk

For Gary

A trick of the night ...

Night. Everything is dark. Dark as dreams.

Not quite everything. If you look very carefully, there's a single purple dot, shining in the distance.

The dot starts to revolve and to grow. At first it looks like a shiny loaf of purple bread, but as it spins nearer, you can see it's not. It's a house, a tiny one. Bright purple with a green front door.

The house hovers and hums, and it is glowing. Grass grows in front of it and flowers shoot out around it, giving off a strange scent of sparklers and hot chilli peppers.

Suddenly the house stops spinning. The front door opens and a girl steps out. A tall thin girl with silvery-white hair and eyes so deeply violet that they match the walls of her little house perfectly.

She smiles and lifts her long arms in welcome.

'Hello, Best and Only,' she says. 'Sorry I've been so zooming long!'

She flashes her wonderful eyes and several strings of

1

violet stars fly up and dance in front of the girl, twining their way around her.

There's a skittering scattering sound. The girl looks up and laughs as she sees the strange yellow hail pouring down on her house and on her head. She opens her mouth and catches a blob of it on her long tongue. She munches the hail as if it is the sweetest, most delicious treat, like popcorn.

'Home, sugary home!' she says, and the sweet hail falls faster and harder, rattling on the roof of the house. It pours down so hard that the girl is covered in a thick, rustling blanket of hailstones. Her shining eyes are the last things to disappear.

But even when she is completely hidden, her laughter rings out quite clearly.

It is the merriest sound you'll ever hear.

Chapter One

Martha pushed herself up on her elbows. She needed to get rid of that laughter.

'Quiet!' she said.

She gave her head a vigorous shake and the laughing faded and then stopped.

Martha sank down on her pillow. Now all she could hear was the rain hurling itself at her window. Everything was normal again. The world was back to its true and gloomy self.

The dream had given Martha a warm feeling inside, a feeling that something good was about to happen, a feeling that Opal Moonbaby was coming back. Which was annoying because there was nothing good happening today. And the longer time went on, the more sure Martha was that Opal Moonbaby was never going to come back.

When she thought about all the amazing things that had happened over the summer she could hardly believe they were real. No one else would believe it either if she told them. An alien girl had landed on the Half Moon Estate. An alien girl who could see through things and

read people's minds. An alien girl with a pet called a mingle, who was a mix of six different animals Opal had mixed up herself in the Minmangulator. Who in their right minds would believe that?

Martha would never actually tell anyone the truth about Opal Moonbaby and Garnet. That was a secret. The only person she could talk to about Opal was her brother, Robbie. They had to wait until they were on their own, which often wasn't until Mum turned their light out, when they were supposed to be going to sleep. Then Martha would lean down from the top bunk and say, 'Do you miss her?' or Robbie would tap the base of Martha's mattress with his telescope and say, 'Wish Garnet was here'. They would spend ages remembering all the things that had happened and puzzling over where Opal and Garnet could be now.

They hadn't seen them since the Fiesta at Pirate Planet, when Opal had failed her challenge. She had thrown away her chance of getting a Carnelian Independence Award on purpose so that she would be banished to Earth for a whole year, so that she could spend that year with Martha. They had ridden the roller coaster together, holding hands and shouting at the tops of their voices. *Best and Only Friends, until the end of time!* Martha had never been so happy.

Then Opal had disappeared.

Martha had looked for her often. In the empty flats where they had first seen her, in the play pipe where they used to hang out together, in all Opal's favourite hiding places in the park. She had even looked in the wheelie bins, but there was never anything in them except black bags, full of stinking rubbish.

Robbie thought she had been kidnapped by aliens, or rather, *other* aliens, since Opal was an alien herself. Martha thought Opal's Uncle Bixbite had taken pity on her and let her return to Carnelia after all. She did think Opal might have tried to say goodbye though, or at least left something behind that Martha could remember her by. If it wasn't for Robbie knowing about Opal too, if it wasn't for the fluttering that began in her chest every time she thought of her, Martha might have started to believe she had imagined her, imagined the whole thing.

The leaves were only just falling from the trees outside but the summer holiday already seemed like a hundred years ago to Martha.

As she picked up her school uniform from the chair, she noticed that Robbie wasn't in bed. Normally when Martha got up he was still buried under his duvet. He liked to stay there until the last possible minute, until Mum threw the duvet off him and told him to get out of bed or else.

This morning, though, the familiar Robbie trail on the floor showed that he was already up. His pillow, pyjamas and *Ahoy, Matey!* pirate magazines lay across the floor. He always lobbed them there from bed before hopping out and leaping from pillow to pyjama bottoms to a double-spread of Evil Blackbeard, on his way out of the room. Robbie never stepped on the actual floor because if he did that a killer shark would grab him and pull him into the deep and snap him in two like a biscuit. That's what Robbie said anyway.

She found him in the living room with his pirate hat on. He had a black patch over one eye and his old toy telescope glued to the other. He was moving the telescope slowly over the Half Moon Estate, scanning the play area, the paddling pool and the park.

'What's out there?' said Martha.

'Nothing,' said Robbie. 'Yet. But something's coming. Just you wait.'

Outside the road was jammed with rush-hour traffic. Martha could see a few early morning dog walkers, a cat going to the toilet in the play area. And Alesha, huddled under a frilly umbrella, on her way to A Cut Above, the hairdressing salon where she and Mum worked. There was nothing unusual.

'What are you on about, Robbie?'

He lowered the telescope for a moment and looked at her. 'I had a dream.'

'A dream?' repeated Martha.

'Yup. The most amazing dream. There was this incredible shiny house.'

'A house?' Martha felt her fingers beginning to tingle. 'What colour was it?''

'Purple,' said Robbie. 'And spinning.'

'Spinning?' Martha laced her fingers together, pressing out the tingles as she listened.

'Right, and it had this bright green front door, and guess who came out of it?'

'Can't,' said Martha although she could really. She was beginning to feel light-headed.

'Opal Moonbaby!'

Martha shook out her hands and frowned. 'So?'

'So she came out and she spoke to me. She said,

"Hello, Cucumber Hero." Remember how she called me that after I hit the milkman with a cucumber in the mini-market?'

Martha nodded.

'She said, "Sorry I've been so zooming long," and then these stars came out of nowhere and it started raining. And Opal was eating the rain, and you'll never guess what it was made of!'

'Popcorn.' Martha sat down heavily on the arm of the sofa.

'Hey! How did you know?'

Martha spoke very quietly. 'I had the same dream.'

'You're kidding!'

Martha shook her head. 'Only she didn't say "Cucumber Hero" in mine. She said "Best and Only".'

'Wow!' said Robbie. 'That is so random and immense!' Random and immense were his new top favourite words. He put up his telescope again and waved it at the sky. 'That proves it. She's definitely coming back. Today must be the day.'

'It doesn't prove anything,' Martha said. She was wishing she hadn't let on about having the same dream. Now Robbie's hopes were raised and she knew there was nothing worse than having your hopes raised and then smashed to smithereens. It had happened to her too many times already. Deep down, she knew it was pretty amazing that they'd had an almost identical dream. But she hated having little seeds of hope sprout in her brain only to see them trampled and crushed again and again. She wasn't going to let this seed get going.

'It's a coincidence!' she said, surprised at how fierce

she sounded. 'We dreamed the same thing because we ate the same food and watched the same TV programme last night. Maybe it was something to do with Mum's pasta bake. It's nothing to do with Opal. It's just a . . .' She raised her arms, searching for the right word. 'It's just a fluke!'

Robbie banged his telescope on the window sill. 'Martha! Why do you have to spoil everything?'

'I don't want to spoil *anything*. I only—'

Robbie cut her off. 'Yes, you do. You *do* want to spoil things. You want to make everybody as miserable as you are. Well, I still believe in Opal, even if you don't.'

He stomped over to the table and poured himself a massive helping of cereal, sloshing the milk over the side of his bowl.

Martha went to the counter, keeping her back turned as she buttered a slice of bread.

'Everything OK?' said Mum, coming out of her bedroom and slipping her feet into her shoes.

'Fine,' said Martha and Robbie at the same time.

'Oh, good,' said Mum. She threw her favourite haircutting scissors and an energy bar into her handbag. 'Now hurry up, you two. Teeth, hair, book bags. Let's get to school, shall we?'

Martha brushed her teeth so hard her gums ached and she dragged impatiently at the snags in her hair. In the lift on the way down to the ground floor, she stood as far away from Robbie as possible. Normally they had a fight over who was going to push the lift buttons, but not this morning. Mum looked quite pleased to have the chance to push the buttons herself for once. She hummed and chatted all the way to school about this and that: the weather, the whereabouts of Robbie's missing school tie (he'd given it to Opal during the summer holiday), the new recipe she was going to try out at teatime. She went on and on as if everything was absolutely fine.

But everything was far from fine.

Chapter Two

'*A hem!*'
Martha jumped and dropped her pencil.
She'd been staring out of the window, thinking about
Opal again. She'd completely forgotten about the maths
test she was supposed to be doing.

'I see the joys of decimal points have escaped you,
Martha.' Mrs Underedge was standing next to her, so close
that the thick wool of her trouser suit brushed Martha's
arm. 'Or have you already completed your worksheet?'
She tapped the paper with one neatly trimmed fingernail.

Martha had only filled in one answer. 'Not quite,' she
said. She picked up her pencil and began to work.

'I should have thought,' said Mrs Underedge as she
patrolled the classroom, 'that you would all be eager
to tackle today's mathematical challenge. As you know,
Merry Class, we have a great deal to do this term,
especially if we are to find time to rehearse the junior
school play. You all need to . . . *knuckle down.* Isn't that
right, Martha?'

Martha was writing furiously, not thinking about her
answers much at all. She wished she could stop thinking

about Opal all the time, but every time she tried to put her out of her mind, she crept back in again. She was always imagining she saw her too. In the mini-market, outside their block of flats, in the park. Everywhere. She felt stupid. She felt like giving herself a big fat kick under the table for being such an idiot.

Mrs Underedge was standing in front of her again. 'I said, isn't that right, Martha?'

'Yes, Mrs Underedge,' said Martha, her pencil coming to an abrupt halt in the middle of a number eight.

'And what is it, Martha, that I am right about?'

Martha didn't know what Mrs Underedge was right about. She looked round. Most of the other children had finished their worksheets. They were all looking at Martha. Jessie Bailey, who was sitting near the front, mouthed something at her.

'We all need to . . . snuggle down?' offered Martha uncertainly.

'Thank you, Jessie, for your efforts on Martha's behalf,' said Mrs Underedge without even turning her head. 'However, I think Martha needs to improve her lip-reading skills. I said nothing about snuggling down. I said, we all need to knuckle down and that includes you, Martha. Now, what do we need to do?'

'Knuckle down, Mrs Underedge,' chanted the class.

'Correct.' Mrs Underedge moved off on her patrol again.

Mrs Underedge was the most boring teacher in Archwell Park Primary, and the strictest. There was a rumour that she had once been much nicer and kinder but no one could remember that. If it was true it must have been a very long time ago.

At lunchtime Martha sat on the wall and watched the

boys racing up and down, chasing a football and yelling at one another to pass it. A brave girl from Reception trekked across, dodging the footballers, on her way to join her friends under the climbing frame. Nearby, a group of girls from Martha's own class sat squashed together on the bench under the tree.

'Coming over?' said Jessie.

Martha shrugged. 'In a bit,' she said. 'Thanks for trying to help me out, by the way.'

'That's OK,' answered Jessie. 'Sorry it didn't work.'

Martha watched Jessie head over to the other girls and perch on the bench. She could have gone along. It wasn't like last term when all those girls would have turned their backs on her, when she would have been excluded from their games, their conversations, everything. They weren't mean to her any more. None of them. Not Chloe, not even Colette. Colette wasn't the queen bee any longer and she didn't speak to Martha in the nasty way she had spoken to her before Opal had shown up and put her in her place.

Martha had even joined the Secret Circle again, but she wasn't a very active member. While the others discussed and schemed, she was always thinking, 'What would Opal say about that?' or, 'I bet that would really make Opal laugh.' She couldn't help it.

Robbie came over, hands burrowed deep inside his pockets. Robbie never normally came near Martha at break time. He didn't like to be seen talking to his big sister in case people said he was a wimp.

'What's up?'

'Only the worst news in the world.' Robbie scowled at the ground. 'Zack's leaving school. His dad got that job in Cornwall and it's definite. I just found out. He's going tomorrow!' He looked as if he might cry. Zack was Robbie's best friend; they did everything together.

'Oh, Robbie, that's terrible.' Martha put a hand on his shoulder but he shook her off. 'You'll really miss him, won't you?'

Glancing behind him, Robbie took Yoyo, his old toy monkey, out of his pocket. He didn't usually bring Yoyo out at school so Martha knew he must be feeling really bad. She watched as he rolled Yoyo into a tight ball and squeezed him into his fist, using his finger to poke the last bit of tatty brown leg out of sight.

'Zack and me were planning to be the cow in the school play. He was going to be the front end and I was going to be the back. We were going to be really funny. Who am I going to do it with now?' he said with a sniff. 'It's not fair. Everyone I like keeps disappearing. First Opal and Garnet vanished, and now Zack's going too.'

'Sorry,' said Martha. She couldn't think what else to say.

'No sign of Opal yet, then?' said Robbie. 'Since the dream, I mean.'

'No,' said Martha. 'No sign at all.'

'She's got to come back today,' he said. 'She's *got* to!'

'Robbie,' Martha said slowly, 'have you – have you ever thought that maybe she isn't coming back?'

Robbie stared at her.

'I mean, do you ever think she might have gone? Gone for good?'

'No,' said Robbie. 'Opal wouldn't just go off. And if she did have to go, she'd find a way of sending us a message.'

'But what if she couldn't? What if something happened to her? If it did, how would we ever find out?'

'Uncle Bixbite could tell us. He could call us on his hydrophone.'

'How? We don't know how to use the hydrophone. Only Opal could do that.'

Robbie kicked at the wall. 'Then he'd send us a comet with a note tied on, or a special asteroid or something.'

'But he hasn't, has he?'

Neither of them spoke for a moment. Around them, the football players argued about a penalty, and the Secret Circle girls exploded into giggles over something in a magazine. Robbie shoved Yoyo back in his pocket.

'That's it then,' he said. 'Everything in my entire life is bad. My whole world is totally disintegrating and imploding. Thanks for rubbing it in, Martha. Thanks a bunch.'

He slouched off to sit alone on the sidelines of the football game. Martha didn't want to hurt his feelings but it was obvious Opal had gone out of their lives for good. The sooner they both started believing it the better.

The bell rang for the end of play.

Disintegrating and imploding, Martha thought. They were Robbie's other two top favourite words, along with *random* and *immense*. It really did feel as if the world was falling apart and caving in on itself at the same time. *Disintegrating and imploding*. Robbie's words fitted the situation perfectly.

She sighed, dropped down from the wall and made her way slowly back to class.

Mrs Underedge was still in the staffroom. Merry Class were supposed to be making a start on their solar system projects, but no one was in any hurry to do that. They messed around and chatted, the noise level rising.

Martha was sitting on her desk, swinging her legs, when Tom Barnes snatched Jessie's pencil case.

'Give that back!' Jessie cried. 'That's my special pencil case from my granny.'

She tried to grab the pencil case but Tom ran round the room keeping it just out of her reach. 'My special pencil case from my special granny!' he mimicked in a silly high voice that didn't sound like Jessie at all.

Martha didn't like seeing Jessie teased but it was still mostly an accident when she recrossed her legs and one of them sort of shot out a bit. Tom fell straight over it and went sprawling on the teacher's table. Everyone cheered, apart from Jessie who shrieked in dismay at the sight of her nice sharp pencils and crayons flying across the floor.

'What on *Earth* do you think you are doing, Tom?'

The room fell silent. Mrs Underedge was back.

'It wasn't my fault, Miss,' Tom protested. 'Martha tripped me. She did it on purpose.'

Mrs Underedge turned to Martha. 'Would you care to explain?'

Not really, Martha thought, but that was the kind of answer that made smoke come out of Mrs Underedge's ears, so instead she said, 'He pinched Jessie's pencil case.'

'Nevertheless, there is no call for violence.' Mrs Underedge looked around at the other children who were all now sitting back in their places. 'Does anyone else have anything to say about this . . . *misdemeanour*?'

Mrs Underedge loved using long words like that and she always paused before she said them, for maximum effect.

No one spoke.

'Good. Tom, go back to your seat and rearrange your jumper, please. Martha, you may stay back at the end of the day to put up the chairs, and you may come over here now and pick up all these pencils.'

Martha crawled under the table and started picking up the pencils.

It wasn't fair. Tom ought to be the one picking everything up. Mrs Underedge never paid any attention to what anyone said; she just decided things to suit herself. Martha had a good mind to stay under the table all afternoon. It would be better than having to listen to Mrs Underedge. She was going on about something right now but Martha wasn't even listening.

She was just reaching out for Jessie's flower-shaped rubber when she saw something that made her freeze, fast, like someone in a game of musical statues.

It was a pair of boots. A pair of silver boots. They were standing next to Mrs Underedge's brown tasselled loafers. Those boots were very familiar.

Martha tuned in to what Mrs Underedge was saying. '. . . As joining a new school is never easy, that you will welcome her . . .'

Martha dared to look a little higher. The owner of the boots was wearing navy-blue trousers, as they all had to for school, but these weren't like everyone else's trousers. At the bottom they were tucked tight inside the boots but after that they started ballooning out like the trousers of an Arabian princess, only to be pulled in again at the waist by a broad silver belt.

'...And,' Mrs Underedge droned on, 'that you will set a good example to our new class member ...'

Martha saw a white shirt, not like her own polo style one, but one with long frilled sleeves that almost covered the owner's pale hands. It had a ruffle down the front where the buttons ought to be, and no collar at all.

'... Only remains for me to introduce you all ...'

That shirt might belong to a pirate, or to a king from centuries ago, or to ... or to ...

'Opal Moonbaby,' said Mrs Underedge.

Martha sat up suddenly and banged her head hard on the table. She didn't feel the pain though as she scrambled out from underneath. Because there, looking back at her, stood the person she had been longing to see.

Opal.

Opal was here!

Martha felt dazed, but not from the bang on the head. She'd been waiting and hoping for this moment for so long. Now that it had come she couldn't take it in. She felt light and strangely numb. Opal was here. She was a little taller perhaps and there was a peculiar roundness to her tummy that Martha didn't remember being there before. She was wearing blue instead of purple but she was still unmistakeably Opal.

Opal Moonbaby. There was no one in the world quite like her.

Chapter Three

Opal was beaming at Martha with her huge violet eyes, hopping from foot to foot, bubbling with enthusiasm, looking fit to burst with joy.

'Opal has come a very long way to be with us,' said Mrs Underedge. 'She hails from . . . *Muckle Flugga.*'

Several people giggled.

Muckle Flugga? How did Opal come up with that? She wasn't from anywhere called Muckle Flugga. She came from Carnelia, but of course she couldn't tell Mrs Underedge that. Muckle Flugga sounded so silly, Martha thought she must have made it up.

'I see no cause for . . . *hilarity*,' Mrs Underedge went on. 'Muckle Flugga is in the Shetland Islands, in the very north of the British Isles. Now, Opal,' Mrs Underedge cracked a slight stiff smile, 'welcome to Merry Class.'

Martha hoped Opal noticed that smile. She should make the most of it. You were lucky if Mrs Underedge smiled at you more than once a term.

'I'm sure you'll soon settle down.' The teacher was staring at Opal's silvery white hair as if she wished that would settle down too. It wouldn't. Opal's hair stood up

in the air like that all the time.

Opal winked. Martha knew she was reading her thoughts because she gave her hair a tweak as if to say, 'Yes, my hair points at the sky and that's that!'

'Now, Merry Class,' Mrs Underedge went on, 'Opal will be feeling rather shy so you must all make allowances. Just as I am making allowances, Opal, for your . . . *interpretation* of the school uniform.' She looked Opal up and down with obvious distaste. Opal was wearing all the right things, but somehow they didn't look right. She was even wearing a school tie. It was the one Robbie had given her in the summer. She had liked it so much she had never taken it off. But the tie had no collar to go round, its knot was in the wrong place, and its tail hung down Opal's back like a long sticking-out tongue.

Martha couldn't understand why Opal wasn't saying anything. She had never known her to keep quiet for this long before. It couldn't last.

It didn't.

'Oh, thank you!' Opal burst out in a voice that seemed much too loud for Merry Class. 'Thank you so much for making allowances for me. That is so extremely marvellously kind of you.' She dropped an awkward sort of curtsey, then grabbed the teacher by the shoulders and gave her a big hug. 'You're so kind to me, Mrs Overedge!'

'*Underedge*,' corrected Mrs Underedge, quickly extracting herself from Opal's grip. She took off her glasses and began polishing them on her jacket. 'Now, let's find you a place to sit . . .'

'And may I say,' Opal went on, 'what an honour it

is to be in Merry Class. I think we are going to have tremendous fun together, don't you, Mrs Otherhedge?'

'Underedge. Have you quite finished?' Mrs Underedge was looking ruffled.

'Not quite,' said Opal, and Martha sensed she was far from finished. A ripple of laughter ran around the classroom and was quickly smothered by a look of ice from Mrs Underedge.

Opal didn't notice. She shoved her hands in her pockets and twizzled round her trousers which seemed to have become twisted during her curtsey. 'I think,' she said, patting her newly plump stomach, 'that I am going to absolutely love being in Merry Class and I'll bet you're a zooming fantastic teacher, Mrs On-the-edge.'

'Underedge,' said Mrs Underedge weakly. 'Now, may we continue, Opal? Or is there anything else you'd like to add?'

Martha knew Mrs Underedge didn't really want Opal to add anything but Opal didn't realise this. If you wanted Opal to do something you had to tell her straight out. Opal couldn't take hints; she didn't understand them.

'Actually, there is something else,' she said. 'And thank you for the reminder. I do need to mend my manners.' She curtsied again, making a slightly better job of it this time, and said in the sing-song voice of someone leaving a party, 'Thank you very, very much for having me, Mrs Udderidge!'

Laughter broke out again in unsuppressed snorts and splutters.

'Quiet!' called Mrs Underedge, her voice rising an octave or so as she backed away from Opal and almost stepped on Martha's feet. 'Ah, Martha,' she said, looking vaguely relieved to see her there. 'Perhaps you'd ... *oblige*

24

us by showing Opal to her seat. You can sit together, by the stationery cupboard, at the back.'

Martha wondered if Mrs Underedge thought sitting next to Opal was some kind of punishment, but right then if someone had given Martha a choice between:

(a) going on an exotic island holiday,

(b) riding over the city in a hot-air balloon, or

(c) sitting next to Opal Moonbaby in school,

she would have chosen (c) every time.

She went over and stood next to Opal. She had thought about nothing but Opal Moonbaby for weeks. She had spent ages remembering all the details of Opal's appearance, her voice, the things she said, everything, but her presence still came as a shock somehow. Her ears looked pointier than Martha remembered, her teeth more jumbled, and her eyes more brilliantly violet than ever. Seeing her mad hair, her cranky outfit, the way she fizzed and bubbled with energy, it was like meeting her for the first time all over again.

A thousand questions jostled in Martha's head. Where had Opal been? What had she been doing? Had she been back to Carnelia? Why hadn't she been in touch? Where had she got hold of that funny school uniform? She could tell by the way Opal's eyes gleamed back at her, the violet of them deepening and lightening, that Opal heard all the questions and was answering them. Sadly, though, it was only Opal who could read minds. Martha would have to wait until they could talk in private to have her questions answered properly.

As if to make up for that fact, Opal suddenly leaned in and lifted Martha up. She lifted her right out of her shoes.

'Where've you *been*?' whispered Martha. She couldn't help chuckling as she breathed in Opal's familiar smell of sparklers and hot pepper.

'Here, there and anywhere,' Opal whispered back. 'Sorry I've been so long.'

Mrs Underedge looked disapproving. 'Is it the custom on Muckle Flugga,' she asked, 'to hug a complete stranger?'

'Oh, Martha isn't a stranger to me,' said Opal, letting Martha back down into her shoes. 'She's my Best and Only Friend. I met her when I first touched down . . . I mean landed . . . I mean arrived. I liked her instantaneously. She's terrific, don't you think?'

'I'm sure,' said Mrs Underedge, not sounding sure at all. 'Now sit down, the pair of you. We really must get on with our topic.'

Martha sat down and pulled out the chair next to her for Opal to sit on. Opal had said she was her Best and Only Friend. Whatever had happened in the weeks she had been gone, Opal still felt the same way about her. She wanted to talk to her so much but talking was never allowed in Mrs Underedge's class. Martha had to make do with watching Opal instead, as she tidied her long legs away under the table, looking as excited as someone who has just been served a giant bowl of ice cream.

Martha noticed Colette and Chloe turning round in their seats and staring at Opal. They definitely remembered her. It was Colette's fault that Opal had been separated from Garnet in the summer. Colette didn't know it but Carnelians had to have their mingles with them at all times; they couldn't survive without them. If Martha hadn't rescued Garnet for her, Opal would have died.

Martha wondered where Garnet was now. He couldn't be far away.

To answer her, Opal lifted one of the many folds in her trousers, revealing Garnet's white muzzle and paws. Martha gasped. So *that* was why Opal was looking a bit on the tubby side. She was hiding Garnet inside her trousers.

Garnet blinked his round owl eyes and Martha reached out a hand to stroke the soft fur between his lynx ears. *'Chigga-chigga-chigga,'* he purred.

'No giggling,' Mrs Underedge snapped. Martha drew her hand back and Opal covered Garnet up again. 'Now,' said the teacher, clicking the lid off a marker pen. 'Let us return to the solar system.'

'Oh, goody gum pops!' Opal cried. 'My best subject!'

Chapter Four

Opal thoroughly enjoyed the lesson. Everyone else enjoyed it too. Everyone, except Mrs Underedge.

'Let's recap for Opal's benefit,' said Mrs Underedge. 'How many planets are there in our solar system?'

'Eight!' shouted Opal at once, with all the enthusiasm of a contestant on a TV quiz show. 'I'm right, aren't I, Martha?' she said, patting Martha's arm.

'That is correct,' said Mrs Underedge. 'Well done, Opal. However, in Merry Class, when we think we know the answer we put up our hands.'

'Got you,' said Opal. 'Message received and under my hood!'

Mrs Underedge looked puzzled but she carried on. 'Can anyone name these eight planets?'

Opal put both hands up high in the air, the way you might if someone was aiming a gun at you, and gabbled, 'Mercury Venus Earth Mars Jupiter Saturn Uranus Neptune.'

'Thank you, Opal. One hand will do. And perhaps you could wait until I point to you before speaking.

'Oh yes, Mrs Oddlesedge,' said Opal, beaming round at the class. 'I'd love to hear the other people's voices. I bet they're lovely.'

'Good. Who can tell me which is the biggest planet?'

Opal's hand shot up again but no one else's joined it.

'Anyone?' said Mrs Underedge. 'What about you, Chloe?'

'Saturn?' offered Chloe.

'No. Tom?'

'Mars, Miss?'

'No. Jessie?'

By this time Opal's hand was up so high Martha worried she might pull a muscle in her armpit. She was keeping her mouth shut tight but little squeaks were coming out, she was so desperate to give the answer.

'Mercury?' said Jessie.

Opal couldn't contain herself. 'No, that's the smallest. It's Jupiter, Jupiter, Jupiter! Jupiter's the biggest. Jupiter's enormous. Did you know that if Jupiter was an empty shell you'd be able to fit more than one thousand Earths inside it and still have room left over for a billion swimming pools and a couple of hundred crates of your bendiest bananas?'

Mrs Underedge was beginning to bristle. 'Quite the expert, aren't you, Opal? Perhaps you'd like to take the lesson for me?'

'I'd zooming well love to!' said Opal, not understanding the sarcasm in the teacher's voice. Bouncing up from her desk, she whipped Mrs Underedge's marker pen out of her hand and started drawing energetically on the whiteboard.

Mrs Underedge was too stunned to do anything for a moment. She stared at Opal's drawing along with everyone else. Martha could see Opal was attempting to draw the solar system but she ended up with something that looked more like a plate of spaghetti.

'Not easy, is it,' said Opal to the class, 'this drawing lark?' She handed the marker pen back to Mrs Underedge. 'You'd probably do a better job than me, Mrs Uds-and-suds. Why don't you have a go?'

'Opal Moonbaby,' said Mrs Underedge, clearing her throat and drawing herself up to her full height. 'For the last time, my name is Mrs Underedge. Un. Der. Edge. Now go back to your seat immediately.'

'Right you are, Mrs Un. Der. Edge,' said Opal. 'Over to you, Sir.' She saluted and strode over to her desk, as the rest of the class giggled, a little nervously this time.

'How am I doing, Best and Only?' she whispered loudly to Martha. 'Do you think I'm blending in all right?'

Martha put a hand over her mouth to stifle the laugh that was bubbling up inside her. If there was one thing Opal wasn't doing, it was blending in. Martha could see by the look on Mrs Underedge's face that her friend was heading for trouble. Opal was enjoying herself so much though and it was so funny having her in the classroom, Martha didn't want to spoil things. 'You're doing well,' she whispered. 'Really well.' There would be plenty of time to explain about school and teachers when they were alone together, later on.

Martha couldn't wait for later on. She glanced at the clock and then back at Mrs Underedge who always seemed to notice when people were clock-watching. To her surprise, Mrs Underedge was looking at the clock as well, as if she too was eager for the lesson to be over.

There was a short silence which Opal decided to fill. 'Come on, Mrs U,' she said. 'What's the trouble? Bat got your tongue?'

'I-I beg your pardon?' stammered the bemused teacher. The other children didn't even dare to laugh this time.

Opal carried on regardless. 'You can't have finished with Jupiter yet, can you? There's so much more to say. The temperature, for instance. It's zooming freezing there, isn't it? It's got an air temperature of minus one hundred and fifty-three degrees centigrade. That's probably too cold for an Earth dweller to even imagine! And there are the rings that go round it, and the storm in the middle that they call the Eye. Oh, and don't forget the fifty moons. And . . . why are you treading on my toes, Martha?'

'OPAL MOONBABY!' Mrs Underedge shrieked, making the entire class jump. Even Opal looked surprised. 'Opal Moonbaby,' Mrs Underedge went on in a quieter but strangled-sounding voice. 'This may be your first day at Archwell Park Primary School but if it wasn't for the fact that the bell is about to ring, I would now be sending you straight to see Miss Brocklebank, the head teacher.'

'Well, that's a shame,' said Opal. 'Because I'd like to see

Miss Brocklebank. I'd like to see her any time. Maybe I could go tomorrow instead.'

Mrs Underedge sighed deeply. 'Very likely,' she said. 'Very likely indeed.'

The bell rang and she sat down heavily in her chair. Normally she kept Merry Class back for at least five minutes after the bell but she didn't seem to have the energy for it today. She sat very still, while everyone grabbed their bags and trooped out. Opal gave her a friendly pat on the back. 'See you tomorrow, Mrs U,' she said. 'Can't wait! I'm the merriest member of Merry Class.'

Mrs Underedge's eyes were glassy; she looked at Opal without seeing her as Opal did a little dance to demonstrate just how merry she was feeling.

Then Opal saw Martha, still sitting in her place. 'Come on, Best and Only,' she said. 'What are you waiting for? We've got a garage-load of catching up to do, you know.'

Martha smiled. 'I've got to do the chairs first.'

'Hokey cokey,' said Opal. 'In that case, I'll see you at home.' She winked mysteriously. Then she adjusted her trousers, which thanks to Garnet had slipped round again, and skipped happily out of the classroom.

Martha hurried to put the chairs up on the tables ready for the next day. She waited to see if Mrs Underedge would say anything about the way she had done it, but she didn't even seem to be aware that anyone else was in the room. She had her handbag on her lap and was rummaging through it, picking out what looked like picture postcards, and muttering.

Martha grabbed her book bag and sped down the stairs, two at a time. She was going to make Opal tell her everything that had happened in the weeks they had been apart. She wouldn't let her budge until she'd told her every single detail.

"Opal's back!" she thought as she ran. And she was so happy she laughed out loud.

Chapter Five

There was no sign of Opal in the playground but Robbie was waiting by the gate. Martha could tell from the way he was standing, all slouched and miserable, that he hadn't spotted Opal yet. She ran over.

'Hi,' she said. 'Guess what!'

'I don't know why he has to look so pleased about it!' interrupted Robbie.

'What?' Martha was confused. 'Who?'

'Zack! He's so chuffed about going to Cornwall. Keeps talking about what kind of surfboard he's going to buy. He doesn't care who ends up in the cow suit with me. I don't think he cares about me at all. Come on. I want to go home.'

He began running along the pavement, his backpack banging against his shoulders as he went.

'Wait,' called Martha, sprinting after him. 'I've got something to tell you.'

A woman had just reached the other side of the road and the pedestrian signal had stopped beeping; its light was flashing amber, about to go green again to let the traffic through. To Martha's horror, Robbie ran into the road without even looking.

There was a big brown vehicle, a lorry or a bus, coming along the road. It was coming pretty fast, fast enough not to be able to brake for Robbie. Without stopping to think, Martha plunged into the road herself. Keeping her eyes on the vehicle which was swerving all over the place, she overtook Robbie, grabbing his arm and making him run even faster than before. They both stumbled up the kerb, fell and landed hard on the pavement.

'What d'you do that for?' Robbie protested.

Martha watched the vehicle go by. It was a sort of giant camper van. You could get camper vans in all sorts of colours but Martha had never seen one like this before. It was covered in shaggy black and brown material, the kind you might expect to see inside, on the seats perhaps, but not on the outside. The material hung all over the van in tassels, even over part of the windscreen. The tassels made it look like a big angry dog that was running but couldn't see where it was going.

As the van careered past Martha caught a glimpse of its occupants. There was a woman driving. She was peering, pale faced, at the road, spinning the steering wheel this way and that, her tongue sticking out as if she was still getting the hang of driving. Her hair, a mass of black, brown and orange corkscrews, swung wildly around her face.

There was a long-haired girl in the van too, squinting at a big map of the road. Martha thought she must be the driver's daughter because she had the same dark, orangey hair. The girl raised her head and gazed out of the window with a blank expression. She had very dark eyes that seemed too large and too round for her white, pointed little face. She reminded Martha of the wolf spiders she had seen on TV, on Mum's favourite nature programme. Although unlike the spiders, the girl didn't have any fangs.

The van veered away, narrowly missing a line of people at the bus-stop. With a shriek of brakes and a spurt of black exhaust fumes, it turned right and disappeared down a side street.

Robbie was still sitting on the ground trying to lick blood off his knee. 'Did you have to knock me over just then, Martha?'

'You didn't want to be *run* over, did you? You should be thanking me. I saved your life.'

'Rubbish,' said Robbie. 'I could have outrun that thing easy.'

Martha raised her eyebrows. She was about to argue with him when she heard a piercing squeal of horror coming from the Half Moon Estate.

'Quick!' shouted Robbie. 'Somebody needs our help. Sounds like they're disintegrating.'

The first squeal was followed by another even louder one.

'Or possibly imploding!'

They rushed round the corner to find out what was going on.

'Oh! Oh no! No, no, oh my mama flipping mia, no!'

It was Alesha, Mum's boss. She was standing outside the back of the salon, squealing hysterically and flinging her arms around, the way she did when she remembered that she was part Italian. She was only a fraction Italian, about one fourteenth in fact, but she liked to make the most of it. She was gasping now and gnawing her knuckles while Mum stood behind her calmly shaking out hairdressing capes.

'Hi, Mum,' said Robbie, sounding disappointed. 'What's up with Alesha? Has she grown another pimple?' It was usually something like that. Alesha liked looking good and if she found a spot or a new freckle on her face, she would moan on to Mum about it for hours.

But it wasn't a freckle or a pimple this time. It was something much more interesting.

'Where on Earth do you think that thing sprang from?' said Mum.

And there it was. Right on the edge of the park.

A shiny purple hut in the shape of a perfect loaf of bread. Its smooth walls glimmered in the sunlight. It had a green door and one window facing into the Half Moon Estate.

'My dream,' murmured Martha. The little building was the exact colour and shape of the one in her dream.

'Mine too,' whispered Robbie. 'It's real. Really, really real!' He looked at Martha. 'She's here, isn't she?'

Martha grabbed his arm. 'Yes, I've been trying to tell you. She came today. She's started school. Robbie, it's so exciting. Opal's in my class!'

Robbie grinned. 'Immense!' he said. 'Told you she'd be back.'

They followed Mum and Alesha over to have a closer look.

Alesha was trying to peer into the hut but its only window was smoky rather than clear and all she could see was her own reflection.

'How'd they put it up so quickomondo?' she said.

'It'll be one of those new German kits," said Mum.

I've seen them on *Canny Creations*. They bring them in on a lorry and a few minutes later, bingo! A whole house goes up.'

'Well, I don't like it,' said Alesha, circling the little building. 'Must be ever so darko in there. That shade of purple turns my stomach. I don't know what this thing is but if you ask me it's a blotto on the landscapio.'

'It's very unusual,' said Mum. 'I like the way it comes with its own ready-made flower bed.' Even though the hut appeared brand new, it already had plants sprouting out from under it, many of them in full bloom.

'What's this, do you think?' Mum bent to lift a flower shaped like a star. 'Strange scent it's got. Some kind of rose?'

'Not a rose, dear lady, but a lily. An Earthgazer lily to be precise. It's called that because it's always gazing at the ground.'

Opal was standing in the doorway, still in her school uniform, grinning from one pointed ear to the other.

'Oh,' said Mum, letting the flower drop. 'I'm sorry, how rude of me.'

Martha didn't think Mum was being half as rude as Alesha, who was now wiping at the window with her sleeve, still trying to see inside. Opal didn't seem to mind.

'Dearly beloved Marie Stephens,' she said, bowing low. 'You are welcome to sniff my blooms whenever you wish.'

Robbie and Martha laughed but Mum seemed puzzled. 'Thank you,' she said. 'How did you know my name?'

'I know your name because I know your two splendid off-springers.' Opal beamed at Martha and Robbie.

'Hello, Best and Only,' she said. 'Hello, Cucumber Hero. Sorry I've been so zooming long!'

Martha and Robbie stood frozen to the spot, remembering. Opal had said exactly those words in their matching dreams.

Opal turned back to Mum. 'I am Martha and Robbie's spanking new schoolmate. And if it's tickety boop with you, Marie Stephens, I should love to invite them in to my humble swelling place for afternoon teatime.'

Mum looked baffled.

'This is Opal Moonbaby,' said Martha. 'And she means her dwelling place, not swelling place.' Opal was always getting expressions wrong; Martha thought it was because she had learned the English language too quickly, in one week. 'Opal came to the Pirate Planet Fiesta,' she went on. 'Do you remember?'

Mum smiled. 'Of course. You're the girl who won the Fiesta fancy dress competition! I'm pleased to meet you properly, Opal, and I'm sure Martha and Robbie would love to have tea with you. You must have tea with us one day too.'

'Is this some kind of house, then?' said Alesha, her arms folded across her chest. 'Are you actually going to live here? Have you got planning permission?'

'I certainly do have permission,' answered Opal. 'From the highest authority, in fact.' She pointed at the sky and beamed at Martha and Robbie. Martha knew she meant her Uncle Bixbite had given her the permission. He was very high up indeed, all the way up on Carnelia.

'Hmmph,' said Alesha. 'Well, I never saw anything about it in the Council News.' She turned on her heel. 'Come on, Mariella,' she said to Mum. She always called

Mum 'Mariella'. She thought it sounded more Italian than Marie. 'We can't hango abouto here any longer. We've got head refurbishments to perform.'

Mum winked. 'Home by six o'clock, you two,' she said and followed Alesha back to the salon.

Martha and Robbie and Opal stood around with goofy smiles on their faces. None of them said anything at first. Martha had waited for this moment for so long. Now that it had come she felt almost shy.

'I'm so pleased you're here, Opal,' she said finally.

'I'm pleased too,' said Opal. 'I'm thrilled to my pits!'

'This is so immense!' said Robbie.

There was another silence. Martha broke it, saying softly, 'I'd begun to think you weren't coming.'

'Not coming?' exclaimed Opal. 'Of course I was coming. I was always zooming coming!'

'I knew you were,' said Robbie. 'And once Martha and I both had that dream about your house, I was one hundred per cent totally certain. Or I would have been if Martha hadn't tried to talk me out of it.'

'You had a double dream?' said Opal. 'About the Domestipod?'

'Yup,' said Robbie. 'If that's what it's called. We dreamed about it last night and now it's actually actually here.'

'Yes, well, double dreams are important,' said Opal. 'There's always wit and wisdom in them.' She turned to Martha. 'You should never ignore a double dream, Best and Only. Double dreams are omens of the future.'

To her surprise, Martha felt tears come into her eyes. One of them spilled over and trickled down her cheek. Opal noticed it at once. She came over and touched it.

'Why is your face leaking, Martha?' she said, examining the damp blob on the end of her finger.

'She's crying,' said Robbie. 'Human girls do that all the time. They don't even have to have a reason for it.'

Opal gazed at Martha with a puzzled expression, as if she was confused by the blurred jumble of thoughts she saw in her head.

'There is a reason,' Martha protested, wiping the rest of the tears away. 'Of course there's a reason.' But she couldn't say what the reason was. She was so happy to see Opal again, so relieved that she was back and so embarrassed that she hadn't believed in the double dream. All those feelings of happiness and relief and embarrassment had just got themselves rolled into one big overwhelming feeling and that had made the tears pop out. It was too complicated to explain so she shrugged and said, 'I've stopped now anyway.'

'In-teresting,' said Opal, narrowing her eyes at the tear on her finger as if she was some big detective. 'Very in-teresting.' She reached into a small pocket on her shirtsleeve and took out a tiny book. She dabbed the tear onto one of the pages. It made a damp splodge on the paper. Without further explanation, Opal put the book back in her sleeve pocket.

She spread out her long arms. 'Now for goodness' sake, Earthlings, stop doodling on my doorstep and come in. I want to show you round!'

Opal skipped through the open doorway of her tiny purple house, and Martha and Robbie followed her inside.

Chapter Six

Once they were inside the Domestipod, Opal glanced at the doorway and the green door slid closed behind them. She clasped her hands together. 'Home, sugary home!' she said. 'Uncle Bixbite built it for me. What do you think?'

Martha and Robbie looked around. The Domestipod consisted of one oblong room. The building was purple on the outside, but inside everything apart from the green front door was a sort of metallic pink. Not just the walls but the floor too, and the ceiling. Even the windowpane was tinged with pink. Every surface was coated in a hovering pinkish haze which moved forward and back like the smallest of waves lapping on a beach. The walls seemed to move as well, curving and easing themselves outwards, as if the Domestipod was stretching itself to make more room for them all.

'It's almost as if it's alive,' said Martha, wafting a hand through the pink cloud that floated above her head.

Opal didn't say anything to that but her violet eyes gleamed.

'This is wicked,' said Robbie. 'I feel like I'm standing

inside a marshmallow.' He sneezed. 'Hey, Opal,' he said, 'Where's Garnet? Don't tell me you've left him behind – *achoo* – on Carnelia.'

'Couldn't do that, Allergy Boy,' said Opal affectionately. She pulled Garnet from her special school trouser pocket and handed him to Robbie who sneezed some more. Garnet always had that effect on him.

Garnet was a bit squashed, he'd been tucked away in Opal's trousers for so long. His lynx ears flapped up and his flying-fox wings stretched out like pop-ups in a picture book. He looked as delighted to see Robbie as Robbie was to see him. They rubbed noses and Garnet didn't seem to mind at all that Robbie sneezed all over him. Martha thought maybe mingles liked that sort of thing.

As Robbie and Garnet rumbled and purred at one another, Martha took another look at the room. 'But you can't live here, Opal,' she said. 'It's completely empty. Where's the bed? Or the table? There's nothing to sit on. This is worse than the flat you squatted in during the summer holiday. At least that had a cupboard.'

'Yes, it's not very comfy, is it?' said Robbie, stroking the hairs on Garnet's ears.

Opal smiled knowingly. 'The Domestipod may look empty but it's got hidden deepnesses. Watch.'

She flashed her eyes at the wall to her left. A hatch opened and a set of three giant purple beanbags came trundling out, knocking Robbie backwards and then catching him again. Garnet took off for a moment, flapping his wings, and then settled himself down again on Robbie's lap. Robbie wriggled around in the beanbag. 'This is more like it,' he said.

Opal flashed her eyes to the right. A stream of silvery netting sprang out of the wall, leaped across the room and attached itself to the opposite wall. It swung from side to side and then came to rest in the shape of a perfect hammock. A second, smaller net fluttered out and suspended itself below the first. It was another hammock, a miniature one, and just the right size for Garnet.

Opal looked up and a silky light shade in the shape of a half moon unfolded itself. The light inside it came on and a group of blue stars began to circle it.

'That's so pretty!' said Martha, sitting down on a beanbag. 'Now it's looking much more like home.'

'There's no space like home,' said Opal, tapping her nose with a finger.

'But where are your clothes?' asked Martha. 'Where do you wash?'

Opal winked one eye and a clothes rail shot into the room. It was full of the purple suits that Opal usually wore. She winked the other eye and the rail shot back again, hangers clattering. It was replaced by a large shower cubicle decorated with clouds which trundled towards them. Water poured down inside it, accompanied by tinkling music. After a moment the flow of water stopped, the cubicle went into reverse and the music faded away.

As soon as the cubicle was gone, a tongue-shaped tabletop stuck itself out. It had three stools attached to it which bobbed about on the long springs that held them in place. On top of the table was a large glass goblet filled with little green balls.

'Time for tea!' announced Opal, bouncing up and

down on one of the stools. Martha and Robbie joined her at the table while Garnet flew up to his hammock.

'Hold out your hands,' ordered Opal. She cupped her own hands in front of her. Martha and Robbie did the same. The green balls in the goblet began to jiggle and whirl around. Two of them broke free and flew out of the neck of the goblet into Opal's hands. Two more balls followed, landing in Martha's hands, and another two went to Robbie. They looked like sweets and they were warm.

'Extenzzorellagob!' said Opal. 'Or as you say in your English, bottoms down and up the hatch!' She opened her mouth, threw in two of the balls and swallowed them whole. Robbie said, 'Yay, sweets!' He put both balls in his mouth at once and started chewing.

Martha put one round ball to her lips and licked it. It didn't *taste* sweet. It didn't taste of anything.

Robbie spat a green gooey mess into his hand. 'That. Is. Not. Nice.'

'Thought you'd say that,' said Opal. 'Uncle Bixbite has kindly given me a year's supply of these scoff capsules but I think I might just keep them for emergencies. How about a good old Earthly afternoon tea instead?' She glanced at the floor and a trapdoor snapped backwards. A big basket of groceries perched on a pedestal rose up to the level of the table.

'Where did this lot come from?' asked Martha.

'Ah,' said Opal. 'Thought you might ask me that.' She took a purple purse from her pocket and flicked it open to reveal a wad of rolled-up five and ten pound notes. 'Uncle Bixbite gave me this too. He didn't want me spending a whole year on Earth without coins or paper cash notes. I know all about shopping now, thanks to you, Martha. I can do pounds and pence and make change just like that.' She clicked her fingers. 'I'm the mini-market's best customer. I went in there earlier and shopped till I popped!'

'And there wasn't any trouble?' said Martha, remembering Opal's last visit to the mini-market. She hoped she hadn't let Garnet ride to the cash till on the conveyor belt this time. She hoped there hadn't been a scene.

'Not at all,' said Opal, snapping shut her purse. 'The whole thing went very smoothly. It was as smooth as a lady's bottom.'

'*Baby's* bottom!' corrected Martha and Robbie together.

'Hey! You've got Space Nuggets!' Robbie exclaimed, seizing a carton of cereal. He ripped it open and knocked back a handful of the mini spaceships and asteroids. 'Mum only lets us have this on special occasions,' he said, munching happily. 'It's really bad for us!'

Martha realised that all their favourite treats were in the basket. Opal had obviously collected it just for them. She hummed to herself as she watched them tucking in to cheesy puffballs, oat bars and chocolate twists. After a while Opal picked out a packet of popping corn, opened it and tried a couple of kernels. 'Ow!' she said, clutching her jaw. 'You can't like these. They're stone hard!'

'They're rock hard,' explained Martha, 'because they're not cooked yet. You have to heat them up with butter and sugar, or salt.' She glanced at the scoff capsule dispenser. Could we cook them in there?'

'I should jolly well think so,' said Opal, and she poured

the entire pack of popcorn into the glass goblet.

'How do you turn it on?' said Robbie, looking for a switch.

'No buttons necessary,' said Opal. Martha remembered that Opal had told them there were no switches or controls on Carnelia. Everything was operated by thought patterns instead.

'Yes,' said Opal, tuning in to Martha's mind. 'Or in the Moonbabies' case, *eye* patterns.' She rolled her eyes and the scoff capsule dispenser whirred into life. The popcorn kernels jiggled and started to pop. They pinged off the glass sides of the dispenser, ricocheting to and fro, as Opal added a packet of sugar and half a pack of butter. The kernels began to fly out of the top at great force. A volcanic eruption of freshly cooked popcorn hit the ceiling and showered down, just like yellow hail. It drummed on the tabletop and rattled onto the floor.

Opal, almost hidden by the popcorn hail, stuck out her long tongue to catch a few morsels of the sweet, buttery corn. Her violet eyes sparkled as she munched. Robbie and Martha grinned at one another, remembering their dream. Then, like Opal, they opened their mouths wide, trying to catch as much of the delicious warm snack as possible.

By the time the dispenser stopped dispensing they were all full and sitting in a lovely sticky sea of popcorn. 'This is the life,' Robbie said, licking the tabletop. 'Can we have tea with you every day, Opal?'

'Don't see why not,' said Opal, slapping some cooling cucumber slices on her precious eyes. 'Since I'm here for the foreseeable future.'

Martha thought those words sounded so lovely. Opal

was back at last and she wasn't going away again for a long while to come. Not for the foreseeable future.

'And are you really going to come to school every day?' she said.

'Of course I am. It's all part of the assignment.'

'Assignment? Are you doing another challenge? Like the Carnelian Independence Award?'

Opal lifted one cucumber slice. 'I'm doing the CIA all over again as a matter of factual,' she said. 'I've got to retake it. Only this time there's more to it.'

'Oh dear,' said Martha. 'Was Uncle Bixbite *very* angry with you for failing your CIA?'

'He was. Excessively.' Opal assumed a grave expression and spoke sternly. 'You have jeopardised the good name and future of the entire Moonbaby clan.' She wrinkled her nose. 'That's why I've been in solitary confinement and incommunicado all this time.'

'Incommuny who?' asked Robbie.

'It means she was all on her own and a prisoner,' said Martha. 'I've seen about things like that, on the news. She wasn't allowed to talk to anyone.'

'Not a sausage or a soulmate,' said Opal, with a sigh.

'Were you really on an island called Muckle Flugga?' asked Martha. 'Like Mrs Underedge said?'

'Yes,' said Opal. 'I'd been on Earth so long that my eyes needed an energy top-up. I wasn't allowed to go back to Carnelia for a full recharge, so Uncle Bixbite decided to use one of your Earth lighthouses instead. He adapted it specially. It wouldn't have been powerful enough otherwise.'

'Why did he choose the one on Muckle Flugga?' asked Robbie.

'Because,' said Opal, pouting a little, 'it's the furthest away, loneliest lighthouse in your whole United Kingdom. He did it to preach me a lesson. Garnet and I have spent six of your longest weeks rattling around in an empty lighthouse, soaking up light beams, with no entertainment whatsoever. There's nothing on Muckle Flugga, you know. It's just sea and storms and a few silly puffins.'

'I think it sounds exciting,' said Martha. 'I'd love to go a deserted island.'

'Me too,' said Robbie. 'I like the seaside. I bet there are great rock pools.'

'It might have been exciting,' said Opal, 'If you two had been there.' She launched herself into the air and landed on her back in her hammock. 'If I hadn't had Garnie with me I would have gone stark raving conkers!'

'Bonkers,' said Martha. 'It does sound a bit harsh,' she agreed. 'After all it was only one part of your challenge you failed. You did really well in the rest of it.'

'Exactly,' said Opal. 'He shouldn't be cross with me at all really. Not now that I'm the talk of Carnelia.'

'Are you?'

'I should say so.' Opal sat up and took the cucumber slices off her eyes. 'I may not have passed my CIA yet but I am definitely the first Carnelian to make a human friend who's promised to be my friend for Ever and Always.' She pointed at Martha. 'That's you, by the by-way.'

Martha smiled. 'I know.' She felt herself begin to glow at the idea that there was no other friendship like theirs in the whole universe.

'And now,' Opal said, 'you can't go anywhere on

Carnelia without hearing about me. I'm on every communication breeze that goes by apparently.'

'Communy what?' asked Robbie.

'Communication breeze,' repeated Opal. 'It's a news gust. They're always shooting past. And they're all sizzling with stories about Yours Sincerely. Uncle Bixbite wasn't going to tell me because he was cross, but I twinkled it out of him. I'm the most famous Carnelian cadet there is.' She swung her legs so that the hammock began to sway. 'The Mercurials are super-fed up about that, I can tell you. They're as sick as parakeets!'

'The Mercurials?' said Martha, trying to remember what Opal had told her about them. 'Are they the clan that were trying to win the Carnelian Coronet?'

'The ones that keep their power in their hair?' said Robbie.

'That's them,' said Opal, swinging higher. 'They hate the Moonbaby clan being in charge of Carnelia. They think they ought to have a turn. But they oughtn't. They'd turn Carnelia side-down-up in no time. They'd change Carnelian Law to suit themselves, claim all the best land and Domestipods for their own clan and let the rest of the Carnelians go podless and starve. Mercurials like Mercurials and they don't give two toots for anyone else.'

Talking about the Mercurials was making Opal swing faster. 'Do you know?' she went on, 'Uncle Bixie's got it into his brain that the Mercurials might come to Earth and try to do me a mischief. Can you believe it?'

Martha didn't know what to believe. She did know that Opal's Uncle Bixbite, who held the Carnelian Coronet and made all the rules on Carnelia, was very serious and kingly. She didn't think it would be like him to say something that wasn't true.

'Why would they want to hurt you?' she asked.

'Because once I pass my CIA, I'll be next in line for the Carnelian Coronet. I'm going to inherit it when Uncle Bixie retires.' Opal swung herself so high that the tips of her boots hit the Domestipod ceiling. 'The Mercurials want me out of the way so they can make a bid for the Coronet themselves, the devious little skunk-bags!'

Opal swung so hard then that she flipped head first out of the hammock. Martha gasped but Opal managed to right herself and landed neatly on the ground, putting her arms up in the air like an Olympic gymnast at the end of a routine. 'What a cheeky clan they are!' she said. 'Still, I don't know what Uncle Bixie's worried about. Hair power is very inferior to eye power. And Mercurials are so short-sighted, they couldn't find their way to Earth in a month of Mondays. They certainly didn't find me on Muckle Flugga. Uncle Bixie told me to watch out for their space-dome but there was no sign of it what-so-zooming-ever. No sign of anything else either. Garnet and I were bored out of our tiny behinds.'

Garnet snuffled his agreement.

'You don't think they'd come *here*, do you?' said Martha. 'To Archwell, I mean?'

'Of course not,' said Opal. 'Besides, if any Mercurials did show up I'd spot them, wouldn't I? My eyes would Z-ray them immediately.'

'Wow!' said Robbie. 'And then what would happen?'

'Ah, well,' Opal rubbed her hands together. 'First I'd turn my eyes up to maximum. Then I'd laser through their hair and cut off all their power. After that I'd send a light-glance at their backs and dazzle-kick them all the way back to Carnelia.' She kicked an imaginary Mercurial. 'That'll show those good-for-nobodies. That'll teach them to make a mess with Opal Moonbaby!'

'Fantastic!' said Robbie. 'I hope the Mercurials do come. I'd love to see you blast them back to outer space.'

Martha wasn't so sure. It was clear the Mercurials spelled trouble and she hoped never to have to meet one. Opal was always so relaxed and casual, but Martha knew from experience that things weren't always as straightforward as she said. She decided to find out as much as she could about what was planned for Opal's time on Earth.

'What else does Uncle Bixbite want you to do while you're here? What's the extra part of the assignment?'

'Oh, it's easy,' said Opal. She closed her eyes and began to recite. 'Part one. Make sure you fit in on Earth and don't let anyone who doesn't already know you're an alien know you're an alien. Part two. Go to school every day like an everyday Earth child and do everything that Earth children do. Part three. Compile the Human Handybook.' She opened her eyes. 'See. Nothing to it.'

'What's the Human Handybook?' asked Martha.

'It's a new study of human behaviour. To go with the Earth Manual. So Carnelians who come to Earth will know who they're dealing with.' Opal reached into the pocket on her shirtsleeve and took out the tiny book and a stubby pencil. 'Shouldn't take long to write. I'll have it done and dusty in no time.'

Martha didn't think the book looked big enough for a study of anything.

'Yes it is,' said Opal, reading her thoughts. 'Uncle Bixie says human beings are very simple life forms, not much more complicated than those blobby things you have in your oceans.'

'Jellyfish?' offered Robbie.

'That's the fellas,' said Opal. She flicked the book open. 'Look, I've already got cheesy puffs, Space Nuggets and tears. There can't be much more to humans than that, can there?'

'There isn't,' said Robbie, forcing down a few bits of popcorn he'd found on the floor. 'Only TV, football and pirates. That's all we do really. Apart from picking our noses and tickling each other.'

'Picking and tickling,' said Opal, writing them down.

Martha thought there was probably quite a bit more to humans than the list Opal and Robbie had come up with. She didn't say so though because she didn't feel like being the odd one out.

'All right,' she said. 'Then I'll look after you at school. I'll help you fit in.'

'Yes, and I'll look after Garnet,' said Robbie, tickling the mingle under his chin.

'Thanks, Earth dwellers,' said Opal. 'But I won't need any looking after. I shall blend in to human life easily. I'll be totally incognito, just like any old pebble on your pebbly beach.'

Martha smiled. Opal had been in Archwell for one afternoon and she'd already attracted plenty of attention. She was never going to be "any old pebble". She was far too interesting. Martha slipped her hand into Opal's and squeezed it. 'I'm so glad you're back,' she said.

'Me too!' said Robbie.

'I know!' Opal cried. She squeezed Martha's hand in return, sending pins and needles dancing up to her elbow. 'And I'm glad to *be* back. I'm thrilled to pieces. In fact, I'm absolutely over the prune! Come on, Earthlings, let's have a group huggle.'

But instead of embracing them, Opal opened her eyes very wide and, to Martha's amazement, violet stars streamed out of them. The stars blew around the room like bubbles, then began to link together into one long shining violet string. The string looped itself around Robbie, Martha and Opal, encircling them in a starry hug.

'I remember these stars!' Robbie shouted. 'They were in the dream too! Weren't they, Martha?'

Martha grinned and nodded. She didn't know what would happen next, she couldn't even guess, but as the stars shimmered around her there was one thing she knew for certain about the future. It wouldn't be dull. Not with Opal Moonbaby in it.

Chapter Seven

When she got home Martha was desperate to go to her room and think about everything that had happened, but she had to wait while Mum quizzed her and Robbie about Opal. Where was she from? What were her parents like? Was her house really one of those ones that came in a kit from Germany?

The questions were really difficult. They both knew they mustn't give anything away about Opal being an alien, not even to Mum. Robbie kept frowning and scratching his head and saying "Um" and "Well," and "You see," while Martha answered as best she could.

She said Opal was from Muckle Flugga, which was true in a way since she had just come from there. Mum was surprised that Opal didn't have a Scottish accent but Martha said she thought people spoke differently in the Shetland Islands, and Mum seemed satisfied with that.

Martha couldn't tell Mum anything about Opal's parents. It occurred to her that she didn't even know if Opal *had* parents. Instead, she told her that she had met Opal's uncle and that he was very handsome and wore a dark-blue suit. That was all true really. Uncle Bixbite had only been a hologram the first time she saw him, but she had met him in person at Pirate Planet. He was very elegant and grand, and a tiny bit scary.

Then Mum wanted to know what Uncle Bixbite's job was. Martha was trying to think of a normal type of job to give him when Robbie blurted out, "Astronaut!"

'Really?' Mum's eyes lit up with curiosity. Martha worried the questions would get even harder and she would have to make up lies but all Mum said was that she thought an astronaut might have owned a bigger house.

Luckily Mum stopped asking questions then because she noticed all the head-scratching Robbie was doing.

'Robbie,' she said suspiciously. 'Have you got nits?'

Robbie stopped scratching instantly. 'Course not,' he said. Head lice loved Robbie's hair and there was nothing he hated more than having them combed out. He stretched and yawned noisily. 'Oh, I'm tired! I think I need an early night.' He made a speedy getaway to the bedroom.

'Hmm,' said Mum. 'I'm afraid Robbie might be in for the Big T.' The Big T was what they called the treatment Mum gave Robbie when his nits got really bad. Then she took him to the salon and used the clippers on him, on the number one setting. The Big T got rid of all the lice and nits straightaway, but Robbie always made a huge fuss about it.

'That's something to look forward to, then!' Mum smiled wryly at Martha and went to the sink to finish off some washing-up.

'Mm. Think I'll go to bed too' Martha said, eager to get away in case Mum changed the subject back to Opal again. 'See you in the morning.'

Robbie was sitting up in the bottom bunk with Yoyo, counting his nail clippings. He'd saved all his fingernail and toenail clippings since last Christmas and now had quite a big collection.

'I've got a hundred and thirty-seven,' he announced proudly.

'Yuck,' said Martha.

'But nice yuck,' said Robbie, pouring the clippings back into the playing-card box he was using to keep them in. He yawned and lay down. 'It's good Opal's here, isn't it, Martha?'

'Very good,' said Martha.

'Maybe now things won't disintegrate and implode so much.'

'Maybe not.'

Robbie yawned again. 'Maybe the new boy will turn out to be all right too. Maybe he'll be a bit like Zack.'

'I didn't know there was a new boy.'

'There is,' said Robbie. He could hardly speak now for yawning. 'He's called . . . he's called Perry. He's starting . . . tomorrow . . . Mr Morris . . . says.'

'That's great,' said Martha. 'I hope you like him.'

But Robbie's eyes were closed. He was already asleep.

Martha couldn't get to sleep. She was too excited. She lay on her bunk staring up at the glow-in-the-dark stars on the ceiling, her head buzzing with everything that had happened. Tomorrow Martha would be able to show Opal all round school, introduce her to people, show her how to act in the dinner hall. Everything. That was so incredible, Martha felt the need to give her arm a pinch to make sure she wasn't dreaming.

Then she remembered she could do something better than pinching. She pushed back her duvet and slipped down the ladder from the top bunk and over to the window.

It was dark outside, especially over by the park, but she could just make out the humped shape of the Domestipod. It was definitely still there.

'Night night, Opal,' Martha whispered. 'Sleep tight.'

The Domestipod lit up suddenly and glowed back at her. She wasn't imagining it. It glowed once, twice, three times. A warm pinky-purple glow, almost as if it was winking at her, saying goodnight back. It was a special message to her from Opal.

The glowing of the Domestipod made Martha feel that she was glowing too. From now on everything was going to be perfect.

Chapter Eight

Martha sat at the kitchen table, sucking the lid of her pen. It was still dark outside and even Mum wasn't out of bed yet. Martha had been too excited to sleep any longer so she had decided to get up and write a list of Tips and Pointers for Opal. Opal was going to need some clues as to how to behave on Planet Earth. In particular she was going to need help with how to behave in school. As an experienced human being and Opal's Best and Only Friend, it was Martha's job to help with the details.

She had three Tips and Pointers so far.

1 Don't read minds. People don't like it. Especially teachers.
2 Don't use your brain dictionary. No one else has one and it will attract attention.
3 Don't let Garnet out of your pocket. No pets allowed in school!

She stopped sucking her pen lid and added a fourth tip. Possibly the most important one of all.

4 **Never, NEVER** look through things that humans can't look through. That can get you into **BIG TROUBLE!!!**

It had been incredibly funny when Opal first demonstrated her ability to see through things by announcing what type of underpants Robbie was wearing, but Martha could imagine other people getting cross if Opal started seeing through their clothes or into their secret drawers or private diaries. It would be bound to make them suspicious too.

Martha finished the list with:

Tips by Martha Stephens. Your Best and Only Friend.

She folded the list four times and drew an 'O' for Opal on the front. They had been doing illuminated lettering at school and she illuminated Opal's 'O' with her own design of curling leaf tendrils and shooting stars. Then she tucked the list of Tips and Pointers into the front pocket of her school bag, where it would be easy to find. She wanted to give it to Opal as soon as possible.

☆ ☆ ☆

Opal was waiting for them when they came outside. One of her baggy trouser legs had rucked up round her knee, and her new, empty book bag was flapping against her bottom.

'All ready for school, Opal?' said Mum.

'Can't wait!' said Opal. 'It's my first proper day. I've

been looking forward to it all night. Hardly slept a blink.'

'How lovely to see a bit of enthusiasm about school for a change.' Mum turned to Martha and Robbie. 'Maybe you should take a leaf out of Opal's book, eh?'

'They can have a whole branch out of it, if they like,' said Opal.

'Don't worry.' Robbie scratched his head. 'School's horrible. She'll soon realise.'

'Have a lovely day,' Mum said as they reached the pedestrian crossing. She waved them over the road and headed back to the salon.

Opal clapped her hands together like a jolly seal clapping its flippers and began to surge ahead. It was as if she had caught the scent of school in her nostrils and was rushing to get there.

'Wait,' Martha called. 'I need to give you this.' She took the list of Tips and Pointers from her bag.

'What is it?' said Opal.

'It's something I wrote. To help you with school.'

'Far off!' said Opal. 'Thanks, Best and Only.' She tucked the list into her boot and rushed towards the school gates.

'Aren't you going to read it?' Martha was struggling to keep up.

'No time,' said Opal. 'Don't worry though, it'll seep in through my ankle membrane and be in my head brain in no time.'

'Are you sure?'

'Course I'm sure.'

'Opal,' Martha caught her arm. 'I've been wondering. If you don't keep a low profile on Earth,' she lowered her voice to a whisper, 'if anyone does find out you're an alien, if you don't get your CIA this time, what will happen to you?'

'Oh, I don't know,' said Opal with a chuckle. 'I'll probably get sent to live on Drabbar or somewhere. Uncle Bixie hasn't said yet.'

'What's Drabbar?'

But Opal was already steaming into the schoolyard and waving at the other children. 'Ahoy there, schoolmates! Howdy, school pardners!' she said in some ridiculous accent all of her own. 'Are we going to have a super smashing rip-roaring time today, or *what*?!'

Martha saw the looks and barely concealed smiles as Opal passed and stomped happily up the stairs to Merry Class. Martha wanted to go with her but Robbie had stopped to take a stone out of his shoe and she had to make sure he got into school safely.

'Hurry up!' she said, half pushing him through the gate.

'All right,' said Robbie. 'Keep your hair on!'

He stopped dead in front of her. 'Uh-oh,' he said. 'New boy alert.'

'Where?' said Martha.

'There.' Robbie sounded appalled. 'He's a total weirdo.'

'How do you know he's a weirdo?'

'Because I'm looking at him!'

Martha followed Robbie's gaze and saw a boy talking to Miss Brocklebank.

He was short, even shorter than Robbie, and he was wearing a pair of thick-rimmed glasses, much too big for his pale face. Martha couldn't see what colour hair he had because it was covered by a thick brown hairnet which was tied at his neck and hung down his back. The hairnet must have been very tightly elasticated because it came right down over the boy's forehead, squashing down his eyebrows and pushing out his ears.

'What's he doing with tights on his head?' said Robbie. 'Why can't he just have hair like everybody else?'

'I don't think it can really be tights,' said Martha. 'Maybe it's something he has to wear. You know, for religious reasons.'

'Is there a religion that says you have to wear tights on your head?'

Martha didn't know.

'He looks like a creep to me,' said Robbie.

Martha tried not to laugh. 'That's a bit mean,' she said. 'You know what Mum says. You should never judge a book by its cover. Perry might turn out to be really lovely. He might be your next best friend.'

Robbie rolled his eyes.

As Miss Brocklebank led him by, the boy turned towards them and stared. His eyes were very dark brown, nearly black, and there was something in his expression that seemed familiar. But if Martha had seen him before, she couldn't remember where.

Then the boy smiled. The smile was so wide and so sudden it made both Martha and Robbie jump. The smile seemed a bit fake, the sort you might practise in the mirror but never actually use on anyone. It made the boy's cheeks puff and his nose wrinkle and twitch.

'What was that thing he did with his face?' said Robbie when the boy had gone by.

'I think he was smiling at us,' said Martha.

'Looked more like an orang-utan to me, trying to scare off predators.'

'He's probably just nervous. Maybe you could sit next to him,' Martha suggested. 'It might make him feel better.'

'Thanks,' said Robbie, swinging his bag over his shoulder, 'but I'd rather implode!'

Chapter Nine

Mrs Underedge was taking the register when Martha walked into the classroom. Opal called out from the back, 'Come on, Martha, don't be such a slow-bus. There's loads to do, you know. Science and maths and all sorts. We've got a lot on our platters.' She patted Martha's chair.

Had Opal looked at her list of Tips and Pointers yet, Martha wondered as she sat down. She really hoped so.

Opal rubbed her hands together and said in a loud voice, 'Brilliant. Now at last we can get on with our education!'

Tom Barnes sniggered.

Mrs Underedge lowered her reading glasses and peered at Opal, trying to see if she was being serious or not.

'I'm not taking the nicky, Mrs U. You can set your mind to bed on that score,' said Opal, breaking Martha's Tip Number One immediately. *Don't read minds.*

Mrs Underedge didn't reply. She finished taking the register and then said, 'Who can tell me the definition of the word "galaxy"?'

'That's too easy,' said Opal to Martha. 'Let's get the

full answer. That'll give Mrs U a big booster!' Opal flickered her eyes, clicking her way speedily through her brain dictionary.

Bang goes Tip Number Two, thought Martha. **Don't use your brain dictionary.**

Opal put up her hand and, before Mrs Underedge could do anything, said, '*Galaxy: A large, independent system of stars, typically containing millions to hundreds of billions of stars. The four classes of galaxies are—*'

'Thank you, Opal Moonbaby,' said Mrs Underedge. 'But I wasn't asking you so don't shout out.' She turned to Chloe and asked her to answer instead.

Opal may have been keen on getting an education but she didn't seem to have learned her lesson from the day before. She did all the things Mrs Underedge had told her not to. She put up her hand to answer every single question and she spoke before she was told to speak. She interrupted Mrs Underedge constantly and gave her own opinions, whether they were asked for or not. And they weren't asked for. Not even once.

When Mrs Underedge said the planet Saturn, with its many rings, reminded her of a spinning top, Opal said, 'Oh, do you think so, Mrs U? I've always thought it looked more like a little man with his hat squashed down over his face, myself!'

When Mrs Underedge said Mars was red, Opal said, 'Actually it's more butterscotch coloured when you get right up close to it.'

Opal didn't know how to behave in a lesson at all. You were supposed to listen to what the teacher said, or maybe write it down, but she carried on talking to Mrs Underedge as if she was one of her friends. She seemed to think they were just having a little chat.

'You're wrong about Uranus, Mrs U. It does have rings round it, just like Saturn. You can't see them very well, that's all. But don't worry, anyone could make the same mistake. I'm sure you know lots of other stuff.'

Mrs Underedge probably did know lots of other stuff but she didn't seem to know how to deal with Opal Moonbaby. Ignoring her was impossible. She tried getting cross with her but Opal never noticed that she was in trouble. Each time Mrs Underedge told her off, Opal smiled at her as if she'd just offered her a pound to spend on sweets. Mrs Underedge wrote Opal's name on the board seven times for interrupting but it didn't sink in that it was a punishment. 'This classroom has got my name written all over it,' Opal whispered to Martha. 'Isn't it kind of Mrs U to make me feel at home like that?'

Martha just laughed and shook her head. Opal may not have read her Tips and Pointers yet but she was certainly making school much more fun.

At one point Mrs Underedge became so frustrated that she told Opal to sit outside in the corridor.

'Hokey cokey,' said Opal happily, as she went out.

When, quite unasked, Opal burst back in a few minutes later, she actually thanked Mrs Underedge for sending her out. 'I had such a lovely time, admiring all the lockers and coats,' she said. 'Can I sit out there every day, Mrs U?'

Mrs Underedge said she thought that was very likely and attempted to continue with the lesson. She was so flustered, Martha felt almost sorry for her.

Opal whispered happily, 'Mrs U and I are getting on

like a house in flames. I dropped into her mind and do you know, she thinks I'm the sort of girl who might be *excluded*!'

'What?' Martha whispered back.

'*I know,*' said Opal. 'I bet that's something fancy isn't it, being excluded?'

Martha was truly worried now. If Opal wasn't allowed to come to school, she would fail part of her challenge straightaway and Martha would never be able to stay at home to keep an eye on her. She tried to tell her with her thoughts what being excluded really meant but Opal wasn't paying attention. 'I'm hungry,' she said aloud. 'Must be nearly lunchtime. What have you got for your lunch, Mrs U?'

Mrs Underedge was so taken aback that she told her. 'Couscous salad,' she murmured, 'with chickpeas. And a vanilla yoghurt for dessert.'

'Yum,' said Opal, patting her rounded tummy where Garnet was hidden. 'And after lunch, you've decided to cast the school play at last.'

Mrs Underedge spluttered. 'How . . . how do you know what I've decided about casting *Jack and the Beanstalk*?'

'Well,' said Opal, leaning back and putting her feet on the table. 'You've been meaning to do it for ages, haven't you? You just haven't got round to it because you didn't really want the job of directing the school play in the first place. Might as well get it over and dusted with, eh?'

No, thought Martha. Opal definitely hadn't read the list of Tips and Pointers yet. She couldn't imagine Uncle Bixbite being very impressed with Opal's attempt at blending in so far. If Drabbar was the place he had in mind as a punishment for Opal failing her CIA, at this rate she might find herself there pretty soon.

'Just one question, Mrs U,' said Opal, waggling her feet. 'What exactly is a play? Is it some sort of game? I love games!'

Mrs Underedge's eyes were bulging and she looked as if she was having trouble breathing. 'L–lunchtime everyone,' she managed to say, although there were still fifteen minutes to go before the bell. Then she walked straight out of the classroom. She didn't even bother to pick up her handbag.

☆ ☆ ☆

Martha urgently needed to talk to Opal. She needed to make her read the list of Tips and Pointers so that they could put things back on track, but she couldn't get near her in the playground. She was completely surrounded by the rest of Merry Class, jostling for her attention, like she was some sort of rock star. Martha thought it was a good job they weren't allowed to bring cameras to school. If someone took a photo of Opal and the flash caught her eyes, there would be a spectacular and dazzling light show that would be better than fireworks, but completely impossible to explain.

Martha saw a hair elastic on the ground in front of her. She bent down to pick it up and absent-mindedly pulled out two long hairs that were caught in it. She looked at the jumble of legs in front of her. It was easy to see which were Opal's because of her baggy trousers and boots. Martha could see the list of Tips and Pointers too, sticking out of one of the boots. It looked as though it was about to fall out altogether. No wonder Opal hadn't got the tips in her brain yet.

'Give that back, please.'

Perry, the new boy, was standing right next to her. He had his hands in his pockets and he was watching her, his dark eyes blinking through his glasses. Martha realised he must have been there for some time.

'Give what back?' she said.

'My elastical.'

'Pardon?'

'My hair elastical,' said Perry, staring at the round band she still held between her fingers.

'Oh, this,' she said. 'Sure. I didn't know it was yours.' She held the elastic out to him.

'And those.'

'What?'

'Those hairs you've left on the ground for someone to tramplify. They're mine too. Can I have them, please?'

'What?' said Martha in confusion. She looked at the ground, frowning, until she saw where the two long hairs had landed. Picking them up wasn't easy. She had to lick her finger and thumb to make them tacky enough to lift the two strands up off the ground. Then the hairs kept getting coiled round her fingers and it was a job to get them off. She managed it eventually and handed them to Perry.

'OK now?' she said with a smile.

'I'll have to wash them,' said Perry, pocketing the hairs.

Robbie was right. He was a weirdo.

'There you are, Perry!' Robbie raced over to them, speaking very fast. 'Thought you'd got lost for a minute. Try and keep up, will you? So, we've done the classrooms, the staffroom, the music room, the art room, the boiler room and the bogs. I think that's everything. So let's go back . . . Oh, hello, Martha.'

'Hi, Robbie.' Martha was relieved to see him. The new boy was beginning to make her feel uncomfortable.

'Just showing Perry round,' said Robbie loudly. 'Making him feel at home.' He came closer and whispered in her ear. 'I'm only doing it because Mr Morris made me. He said Perry asked for me specially and I had to respect his wishes or something.' Robbie screwed up his face in disgust. 'He's just as bad as I thought. And he keeps asking me if I'm his friend yet. As if! I think he might have brain problems! He's dead creepy and he smells, sort of like a skunk, don't you think? Not that I've ever actually smelled skunk but I reckon he's what one smells like. I never thought I'd say this, Martha, but I actually can't wait to get back to class!'

Robbie didn't have a very quiet whisper and Martha wondered if Perry had heard every word he'd said. She decided he couldn't have though because he just stood there, smiling fixedly at Robbie.

'I'm Martha,' she said to fill the awkward silence. 'Robbie's sis—'

'I know,' Perry interrupted. 'You're Martha. You're Robbie's sister.'

Robbie made a face, as if to say, 'See, I told you he was a creep.'

A roar of laughter went up and the three of them

turned to see Opal disappearing into the dinner hall with her new fan club. Martha had planned to get in first and save a seat for Opal so that they could talk properly. Now she would have to fight to get near her.

'Got to go,' she said. 'Good to meet you, Perry.'

Perry didn't reply. He was already back to staring and grinning at Robbie.

'Do you want to be my friend now?' Martha heard him say as she hurried towards the dinner hall. 'Do you want to play with me?'

'Nope,' was Robbie's reply. 'I'm too busy. I've got some extra maths I've been dying to catch up on.' He scratched his head madly as he ran off. It looked to Martha as if it was Perry, not the nits, he was trying to get out of his hair.

'Wait for me, Robbie.' Perry pushed up his glasses and trotted after him, the strange hairnet flopping against the back of his sweatshirt.

Chapter Ten

When Martha finally made it into the dinner hall, Opal was way ahead of her in the queue. She tried to queue jump but Tom Barnes stuck out his elbow and said, 'Hey, no overtaking!' and several other people glared at her so she had to go right to the back.

As soon as Opal had been served her meal, she was herded away by a group of girls, all eager to get to know her. By the time Martha had collected her lunch there were no places left on Opal's table so she had to go to the next one along. She wasn't hungry. She prodded her jacket potato and beans and watched as Opal chatted happily with her new schoolmates.

They were all laughing and nodding at everything Opal was saying. Even Colette, who had been so awful to Opal in the summer, was looking at her admiringly.

'I like your top,' Martha heard her say.

'Do you?' said Opal, fluffing up the frills that ran down the front of her shirt.

'Yes,' Colette went on. 'Those lacy ruffles are really in at the moment.'

'In?' said Opal, not understanding. 'In what?'

Colette smiled. 'In fashion.'

'Really?' said Opal. 'Thanks for telling me. Fancy me being in fashion! I'm gobstopper-smacked. You could knock me down with the weather!'

Colette and the others giggled. They all looked at Opal with delighted faces, waiting to hear what she would say next.

In a strange way this scene reminded Martha of the day Colette had first arrived in school last year. Everyone had buzzed around her for ages, the way they were buzzing round Opal now. And then Colette had gone and ruined Martha and Chloe's friendship. And their special club.

Opal wouldn't let that happen, Martha told herself. Opal was her Best and Only Friend.

Opal caught her eye then and smiled as if to show that she had caught Martha's thought too. She raised a hand to her mouth and blew her a kiss. Martha touched her cheek; it was moist, as if Opal had really kissed it. She felt better immediately.

'She's funny.'

'What?'

Martha had only just noticed that Jessie was sitting next to her. 'Your friend,' Jessie said. 'She's very funny, isn't she?'

Martha looked over at Opal who was still burbling away while her new companions rocked with laughter. 'Yes,' she said. 'She is.'

'I would have thought she'd want to sit next to you at lunch, on her first day.' Martha wondered if Jessie was teasing her but there was no unkind look in her warm brown eyes, only a sort of gentle surprise. 'I mean, if I'd

80

just started a new school I'd definitely stick with the person I knew best.'

That was exactly what Martha had been thinking. She should have realised that Opal wouldn't be shy like most people but she had been so looking forward to introducing her to everyone, she couldn't help feeling a tiny bit cheated. She didn't want Jessie to know that though.

'It's fine,' she said, trying to sound casual. 'Opal loves meeting new people. I know that. We'll have plenty of time together later on.'

She ate a few beans while Jessie went up for pudding.

'Oh, what a pretty thing!' said Jessie, when she came back. She was holding up a familiar piece of paper and beginning to unfold it. 'Someone must have dropped it.'

Someone had. Opal.

'That's mine!' Martha snatched the now scruffy-looking list of Tips and Pointers out of Jessie's hand. Jessie looked taken aback.

'Sorry,' said Martha, regretting the snatch immediately. 'It's a bit private, that's all.'

If Jessie's feelings were hurt, she didn't show it. She just said, 'That's OK.'

The list was torn in one corner and the dusty imprint of someone's shoe was now covering the 'O' Martha had spent so long illuminating. She put the list on her lap under cover of the table and quickly read through the Tips and Pointers, checking them off one by one. Of the four of them, Opal had broken two already. Why hadn't she looked at the list? Things were going well enough for now, although there was absolutely no sign of Opal blending into the background as she had promised. It was good that the others liked her but Martha wondered if they were a bit *too* interested in her. She was so very different from everyone else; no one would think of her as being just like any other girl. Mrs Underedge definitely didn't. If Opal carried on like this, someone was going to put two and two together and realise that she was an alien.

Oh well, thought Martha, stuffing the Tips and Pointers into her pocket, just as long as she doesn't let Garnet out of her trousers. As long as she doesn't start seeing through things. If Opal kept the last two Tips in mind, everything should still be all right. She would tell her about them when they got back to the classroom.

$$\star \star \star$$

There was no time to have a word with Opal when they got back to class because Mrs Underedge was already there.

'This afternoon,' she said, sitting down behind her desk, 'I am feeling nauseous.'

'I'm sorry to hear that, Mrs U,' said Opal. 'I hope it wasn't anything to do with that sick-pea salad you had for lunch.'

'*Chick*pea,' Mrs Underedge corrected wearily. 'Now, Merry Class, I have decided to make a change this afternoon. Instead of learning about black holes, I will be giving out the parts for our production of *Jack and the Beanstalk*.

Everyone cheered. No one louder than Opal.

'Told you so,' said Opal. 'What's my part going to be, Mrs U? I like the idea of this pretending-to-be-someone-else thing. Colette told me all about it at lunch. I bet I'd be ever so good at acting. It sounds right up my road.'

Martha felt really disappointed that Colette had been the one to tell Opal what plays were. She ought to have been the one to do it. And she doubted whether Opal would really be any good at acting. She was very good at being Opal but she was so very, *very* Opal, Martha couldn't imagine her even pretending to be anyone else.

Mrs Underedge ignored Opal completely and began to read out the names of the characters. 'Jack,' she said.

Opal put up her hand.

'Tom,' said Mrs Underedge. 'You will be Jack for us.' She handed a script to Tom, who looked pleased and proud.

Mrs Underedge walked around the room giving out the rest of the scripts.

'Jack's mother.'

Opal put up her hand again, a little higher this time.

'Chloe.'

Chloe took her script and began flicking through the pages to find her lines.

'The giant – ' Opal kept her hand up –

'will be played by Ravi. And Jessie will be the giant's wife.'

'Whoooh!' crowed most of Merry Class.

'Jessie and Ravi are getting married!' said Colette. Jessie and Ravi both went red.

The parts were going fast now. Martha was beginning to wonder if she would be cast at all.

'Colette will be the hen that lays the golden eggs.' Everyone laughed at that and there was some clucking, mainly from Ravi.

'And Martha will take the role of the singing harp.'

Martha received her copy of the script and saw to her pleasure that she had a solo to sing. She loved singing. She hadn't sung on her own in public before and she was a little nervous but she felt excited too.

Opal had both hands in the air again now, despite what Mrs Underedge had told her the previous day about only using one hand.

'Lauren, Lisa, Henry, Ethan and Kayleigh. You will be the five magic beans.'

Mrs Underedge set down her list. It seemed that there was no part for Opal.

'What about the cow?' asked Colette. 'Who's going to do that?'

'Ooh, ooh, I could do that,' said Opal. 'I can do a really convincing cow call.' She began mooing and lowing and waving her head about.

'The part of the cow,' said Mrs Underedge, ignoring Opal and speaking as if the room was still quiet, 'is to be taken by two children from Cheerful Class. Mr Morris will also be casting the chorus and villagers.'

Opal stopped mooing and burst out, 'And me, Mrs U? What can I be? I want to be in the play too.'

'I'm afraid,' said Mrs Underedge, not looking afraid at all, 'that I don't have a part for you, Opal. You joined us so late in the term. The roles have already been allocated.'

'It's because you think I talk too much, isn't it?' said Opal, breaking Tip Number One again. 'You don't think I'll be able to keep my trapdoor shut.'

'That has nothing to do with it,' Mrs Underedge lied. 'It's simply that the parts have all been taken. Never mind, I'm sure there'll be plenty of . . . *backstage* jobs to

84

keep you busy. Sewing and scene-shifting and so forth.'

Opal couldn't hide her dismay. She didn't even try. She folded her arms on the desk in front of her and laid her head down on them, rolling it around and moaning. Opal wasn't at all a backstage type of person. She was much more the centre stage kind.

Mrs Underedge looked pleased, almost triumphant, as she walked back to her desk. Martha realised what she was up to. She could easily have given Opal a part in the play. She could have invented a part for her, made her a sixth magic bean, or Jack's big sister or anything. She didn't want to because she was trying to teach Opal a lesson. Martha put a consoling hand on Opal's shoulder. Mrs Underedge could be so mean sometimes!

The teacher faced them again, a tiny smile on her face. She was back where she wanted to be, in control of Merry Class. 'Now that we have achieved everything we set out to achieve,' she said, looking at the clock, 'we have a few minutes left for Show and Tell.'

Opal lifted her head. 'Show and Tell?' she said. 'What's that when it's at homeland?'

'It's when you bring something in,' whispered Martha. 'Something special you want to show everybody.'

'Is it indeed?' said Opal. Her eyes widened with excitement, her disappointment about the play already forgotten.

Mrs Underedge was taking out her Show and Tell rota to see whose turn it was – the rota was organised in alphabetical order and they were on the Bs. 'Tom Barnes and Jessie Bailey. Have either of you brought something to show this week?'

Tom and Jessie went to get their book bags but Opal

was busy fiddling with her special trouser pocket. 'At last!' she said, as if she'd known about Show and Tell all along and had been waiting for it to happen. 'About zooming time too!'

Mrs Underedge raised a hand like a stop sign. 'Your surname begins with an M, Opal,' she said. 'Not a B. It won't be your turn until after Christmas.'

Opal wasn't listening. 'Hold on a min, I'll be with you in two clicks,' she said as she struggled with the buttons. The material of her trousers was moving. Martha thought Garnet must be shifting in his sleep.

A wave of horror lurched in Martha's stomach as she saw what Opal was about to do. She was going to bring Garnet out and show him to the class.

There were a dozen, a thousand, a million reasons why Opal shouldn't do that. Pets weren't allowed in school. Garnet was too unusual to pass for an ordinary cat or dog. He had wings! What if he spread them and flew about? What if someone guessed he was from another planet? That would be the end of anyone believing Opal was a human being. That would be the end of her CIA and her time on Earth too. Opal would be sent to a place called Drabbar and Martha would never see her again.

And even if no one guessed Garnet wasn't an Earth animal, Mrs Underedge would still hate him. She would be so angry. She would have him taken away and then Opal would die. He had to be with her at all times or she faded away to nothing. Martha had seen it before. Now it was about to happen all over again. Martha couldn't bear it. 'Opal!' she hissed. 'Stop!'

Opal didn't seem to hear. 'Take a butcher's and a

baker's at this, Merry Class,' she said, standing up and folding back the extra layer of material at the front of her trousers.

'Don't! Opal! No!' cried Martha.

'No! Opal! Don't!' commanded Mrs Underedge.

It was too late.

Garnet flopped out of Opal's pocket and onto her desk. A sleepy heap of crushed fur and feather and fluff. All rolled up like that, he might have been mistaken for an old soft toy or a stuffed cushion. Maybe that's what the others took him for because when he suddenly sat up and shook himself, everyone screamed.

Garnet swivelled his amber owl eyes, licked his white cat fur and sniffed with his pink stoat nose. Martha's only comfort was that he didn't unfurl his flying fox wings too. *'Chigga-chigga-chigga,'* he said.

Mrs Underedge shrieked. 'What is that . . . that beast?'

Garnet turned on his back with his paws in the air, revealing a fluffy tummy marked with orange spots and stripes.

'Ahhhh!' sighed Merry Class. Realising the mingle was friendly they rushed over, all wanting to be the first to stroke him. 'Places, everyone, places!' squawked Mrs Underedge, wading her way towards Opal and Garnet, pushing children to the right and left as she came. 'We do not allow wild animals in school, Opal Moonbaby. This vermin will have to go!'

Opal blinked her eyes and looked up the word 'vermin' in her brain dictionary. She laughed. 'Garnet's not vermin, Mrs Undyundies. He's not harmful to crops or farm animals and he doesn't carry any diseases. Garnet is my faithful and constant companion.'

'No,' said Mrs Underedge. 'No pets in school. No dogs. No cats. No mice. No ferrets. Nothing. It's not allowed!'

Opal put her hands on her hips. 'Well, I'm surprised at you, Mrs U. I was sure you'd understand. You of all people on Earth. After all, you know what it is to be separated from a faithful companion.'

'What do you mean, child?' demanded the teacher. 'What are you talking about?'

'I'm talking about little Letty, of course.'

'Little ... Letty?' Mrs Underedge turned a shade paler.

'Yes,' said Opal. 'You know, your little cat. You can't have forgotten her. You never could. You always keep those photos of her, don't you, in your handbag?'

The class turned as one to look at Mrs Underedge's large brown leather handbag. It sat where it always sat, against her desk. All its zips were zipped up tight. No one was allowed to touch it, let alone open it. No one could possibly know what was inside it.

But Opal could. Martha realised she must have looked into Mrs Underedge's bag and rifled around in there. She hadn't opened it exactly. Not in the normal way. She had simply X-rayed it with her powerful eyes.

NEVER look through things that humans can't look through. Opal had broken Martha's fourth and final Tip. She had only been in school for one day and she had broken every single Tip and Pointer. Martha was stunned. Why wasn't Opal being more careful not to fail her challenge? What did she think she was doing? Was Opal even *thinking* at all?

Mrs Underedge went very white, and then very red. If she had been considering having Opal excluded from school before, she would be considering it a lot harder now. She looked as if she was about to explode.

'Letty was a beautiful cat, wasn't she?' said Opal. She seemed totally unaware of the seriousness of what she had just done.

The class had been quiet before but now it went into a new, extra-silent kind of silence. The kind of silence reserved for very special occasions. It was completely still. Everyone seemed to be holding their breath.

Martha felt she had to do something. Anything. She had to save the situation.

'It's my fault, Mrs Underedge,' she said. 'I unzipped your handbag in the lunch break. I found the photos of little . . . little Letty, and I . . . I told Opal about them.'

Opal leaned across to her. 'Martha,' she whispered. 'That's not even true. Why are you telling that big piggy pie?'

She just didn't get it.

Mrs Underedge erupted.

'Martha Stephens!' she yelled. 'You are a nasty, nosy little girl. You are a disgrace to Archwell Park Primary School. Get out of my classroom at once. Go to the office. Go and see Miss Brocklebank and tell her exactly what you have done!'

'Martha hasn't done anything, Mrs U,' said Opal. 'Don't be such a silly milly!'

The glare with which Mrs Underedge greeted this remark was enough to silence even Opal Moonbaby.

Martha walked slowly to the door, painfully aware that everyone's eyes were following her. She had always dreaded being sent to the office and she had made it all the way to Merry Class without it happening once. She had been told off plenty of times but she had always managed to avoid getting into really big trouble. Now Opal had arrived and her record was shattered.

As she began her lonely walk down the stairs Martha couldn't help feeling hurt. She wanted to look after Opal, she'd promised to do so, but why was she the only one making any effort? Opal ought to be taking her challenge much more seriously.

When she reached the bottom of the stairs, Martha heard someone in Merry Class burst into tears. They were sobbing loud, gasping sobs. She wondered who on Earth it could be.

Chapter Eleven

Martha had been shaking like a leaf by the time she reached Miss Brocklebank's office. But the head teacher hadn't been very cross after all. She seemed much more concerned about whether Mrs Underedge had started work on *Jack and the Beanstalk* yet.

'Excellent news!' she said when Martha told her they'd already been given their parts. 'Now do behave yourself from now on, Martha, won't you?' Miss Brocklebank waved her away. 'Off you go, back to class.' Martha couldn't believe she had been let off so lightly. Miss Brocklebank was very kind but even she ought to have doled out some punishment for the terrible thing Martha had done. Or rather hadn't done, but said she had done.

As she left the office she passed a woman who was on her way in. The woman wore thick glasses and was very short. She was only about the same height as Martha. Martha thought she must be trying to make herself look taller because she was wearing very high-heeled shoes and she had her hair piled up on her head and wrapped in an orange scarf so that it looked like a traffic cone. There was a powerful smell of roses and lavender

91

surrounding the woman, and another smell, like leaking gas. Martha tried not to wrinkle her nose.

The woman didn't notice Martha at first. She was straightening her headscarf. There was something sticking out of the top of it, waving about. For a moment Martha thought it was a tail. It was green and coiled just like a lizard's. The woman was muttering and pushing it down into the scarf which she then twisted and tied into a tight knot. Martha shook her head. She must be letting her imagination run away with her. It couldn't have been a tail. It must have been a ribbon.

Then the woman saw her. She stopped muttering and fiddling with her headscarf and came and stood very close to Martha, making her feel quite uncomfortable. The woman's black eyes were magnified through the lenses of her glasses. Her nostrils were flaring slightly and her nose was twitching, as if she were an animal trying to catch Martha's scent.

Martha wanted to go past her but the woman was blocking the doorway to the corridor. 'Good afternoon, sweetie-heart,' she said, blinking at Martha and smiling, showing a row of very straight, light-brown teeth.

'Good afternoon,' Martha replied, trying not to cough as a mouthful of the gassy perfume cloud hit the back of her throat. She hoped the woman would move aside and let her pass but she didn't, she just kept on staring. The way she stared reminded Martha of Perry, the new boy. He was short too, and wore the same type of glasses. This must be his mother.

To her surprise, the woman suddenly reached out and pinched her cheek, squeezing the flesh awkwardly between her stubby fingers. Martha stepped back in alarm.

The woman gave an odd little laugh and let her go. 'Mustn't be tardy for my meeting,' she said. 'Goodbye for now.' She beetled through Miss Brocklebank's door, letting it shut behind her.

Martha shivered. The woman hadn't been unkind but she felt as if she'd just been sniffed and pawed all over by a strange and smelly animal, like a warthog. This really was turning into the most peculiar day.

The oddest thing was going on when Martha reached the classroom again. The desks had all been pushed back and everyone was sitting in a circle on the floor. Even Mrs Underedge. Martha had hardly ever seen Mrs Underedge sit down at all, let alone sit cross-legged on the floor with everyone else.

Coming further into the room she saw that Mrs Underedge had Garnet in her lap. She was stroking him and dabbing at her eyes with a soggy tissue. Her handbag was lying open in the middle of the circle, its contents strewn about across the carpet. Opal was sitting opposite Mrs Underedge and she was holding up a photograph of a cat.

'Oh, yes,' Mrs Underedge sniffled. 'That was taken on the day of little Letty's first injection. And the one after that, Opal, dear . . .'

Opal, dear? Where did *that* come from? Martha couldn't believe her ears.

'. . . The one after that shows her eating her first bowl of Cutiekins. She did love her yummy yummy Cutiekins!'

Yummy yummy Cutiekins? What had happened to the strict and severe Mrs Underedge they all knew and hated. It was as if she had been replaced by a completely different person. It was definitely her though, because when she saw Martha her voice became much frostier. 'Ah, you're back, Martha. Well, you may go and sit on your own in the corner.'

All the other children cooed over the photographs while Mrs Underedge continued to stroke Garnet.

'Where's Letty now?' Chloe asked.

Mrs Underedge blew her nose. 'She died, I'm afraid.'

'How?' asked Tom. 'Did she get run over?'

'No, Tom. It was just old age. She was eighteen when she left me.'

'That's so sad,' said Opal. 'You must have been heart-smashed!'

Mrs Underedge smiled through her tears. 'I was, Opal, dear. I was.'

Opal, dear again!

'Four years ago,' sighed Mrs Underedge, 'and it still hurts as much as if it were yesterday.'

'That's a dying shame!' said Opal.

'People are very keen on their pets, aren't they?' she observed. She slipped her Human Handybook from her sleeve and jotted something down in it.

'Indeed,' said Mrs Underedge. She lifted Garnet from her lap and placed him on the carpet in front of her. 'And thank you for showing us your little pet, Opal. However, I'm afraid you won't be able to bring him to school any more.'

'Oh, but I have to,' said Opal. 'Garnet and I are inseparable.'

Only Martha knew just how inseparable. She put her hand up.

'We don't want to hear from you, Martha, thank you,' said Mrs Underedge, giving her a cross look.

'Please,' said Martha shakily. 'I've got an idea. We used to have a Pets' Corner in Reception, with a guinea pig in it. Couldn't Garnet be the Merry Class pet?'

'Oh, yes,' cried the others.

'That would be great!'

'Can we?'

'Please?'

'It's out of the question,' said Mrs Underedge.

Then Jessie piped up. 'That's such a good idea, Martha. We could watch his behaviour and study his habits. I bet it would be very educational for us, Mrs U . . . I mean, Mrs Underedge.'

Mrs Underedge stroked the fine lynx hairs on Garnet's soft ears. She seemed to be giving the idea some thought.

'Who's picking you up after school, Opal? Mummy? Or Daddy?'

Opal laughed. 'Neither,' she said. 'I don't have a mummy or a daddy. I don't have any parents at all.'

Mrs Underedge looked horrified. 'Opal,' she said. 'I am so sorry!'

'Don't be,' said Opal. 'It's perfectly standard.'

'Perfectly . . . *standard*?' stuttered Mrs Underedge.

Martha guessed Opal meant it was perfectly standard or perfectly normal not to have parents on Carnelia, where she came from. It certainly wasn't standard on Earth.

'Opal does have an uncle,' she said, trying to be helpful.

Mrs Underedge spoke harshly. 'These interruptions from you, Martha, are becoming very trying. So, Opal,' she said, her expression softening again, 'is your uncle collecting you from school today?'

'What?' said Opal, slapping her thigh and laughing, as if Mrs Underedge had just told her the most hilarious joke. 'Uncle Bixbite, picking me up from school? I shouldn't think so. He's on another planet!'

'He may be a little distracted,' said Mrs Underedge, luckily not understanding. 'But he must look after you, Opal. That is any guardian's . . . *top priority*.'

Martha was getting really worried now. Opal was talking openly about other planets and if she carried on like this she was going to give herself away entirely.

'What Opal means is, her uncle's an astronaut, visiting other planets.' Robbie had planted this idea in Martha's mind and she thought she might as well go along with it. 'He's not always back from outer space in time to pick her up from school.'

The other children all started talking excitedly. Opal had already livened up their day no end with her funny ways and her wonderful pet. Now she had become even more interesting. Anyone with a real live astronaut in the family was well worth making friends with. They shuffled along on the carpet, boys and girls alike, adjusting their positions so they could be closer to her.

Martha hovered on the edge of the group, realising that she was the only one who didn't share the feeling of excitement. The more attention Opal attracted to herself, the more nervous Martha became. At this rate, it would be a miracle if Opal made it through even one full day of school without being revealed as an alien.

Mrs Underedge cut through the chatter with a distraught cry.

'Oh, Opal, don't tell me that you're a . . . *a latchkey child*!'

'A whatty?' said Opal.

'A latchkey child. A child with her own door key who goes home each day and lets herself into a cold house with no one to greet her. Don't tell me you have to make your own tea!'

Opal considered this. 'Course I do. Been doing it since I was three months old. And I put myself to bed too. I don't need any help to get into my hammock. None what-so-zooming-ever.'

Mrs Underedge was shaking her head. 'Oh, dear me! This won't do at all. Opal, tell your uncle that I would like to see him as soon as possible. I'll come to your home. I need to check on your welfare.'

'Right you are, then,' said Opal. 'I'll ask him to check his space log ASAS.'

'ASAS?' said Mrs Underedge.

'Yes,' said Opal. 'As Soon As Sensible.'

As the others giggled, Martha put her face in her hands. She tried to picture Mrs Underedge in the same room as Uncle Bixbite, the two of them having a conversation. It was impossible to imagine.

Martha had been so thrilled to be going to school with Opal that morning. She'd thought it would be fantastic. Now she felt exhausted. She'd been watching Opal's every move, trying to anticipate what she would say, and when she said something strange or did something out of the ordinary, she'd tried desperately to cover for her, only to find that she was the one in trouble. Martha had been waiting so long for Opal to come to school with her. Now that she was here, she was beginning to wonder whether it was going to be so fantastic after all.

Chapter Twelve

It was Saturday. Mum was cutting hair in the salon. Martha, Robbie and Opal were sitting on the pipe in the play area, licking traffic-light lollies and having a meeting.

Opal didn't want to have a meeting at first because she thought it sounded too serious and not at all fun, but Martha insisted.

'All right, Best and Only,' Opal agreed with a sigh. 'You're the boss. I'll do as you say. I'm going to stay in your good bags from now on.'

'Good books,' corrected Martha.

'And them,' said Opal.

The three of them sucked hard on their lollies, trying to work out what to do about Mrs Underedge's request to see Uncle Bixbite.

'He won't come to Earth in person,' said Opal. 'He's far too busy keeping Carnelia in order to come rocketing all this way to talk to an Earth teacher.'

'But he'll have to,' said Martha. 'If Mrs Underedge finds out you're living on your own, she might tell the social services people. You might get taken into care.'

'What's care? Sounds like fun.'

'It's not,' said Robbie. 'We've seen it on the telly. It's when you have to go and live in a big house and wait for ages until someone comes along and likes the look of you. Then they get to take you home and you have to be theirs forever and ever.'

'And you wouldn't be able to keep the Domestipod,' added Martha. 'You might not even be able to keep Garnet.'

'I suppose he might talk to her on the hydrophone,' said Opal, looking over at the paddling pool in the park. Martha had seen the hydrophone in action before. Opal had heated up the paddling pool until it was steaming hot and Uncle Bixbite's watery image had appeared in it, floating about on the surface. He wasn't even all there, not in 3D anyway. Mrs Underedge would be bound to think it was odd, talking to a grown man who was lying down fully clothed in the children's paddling pool.

'I don't know,' said Martha. 'Isn't there some other way she can talk to him?'

'The hydrophone has to have water,' Opal explained, 'or we can't make a proper connection. Not all the way to Carnelia.' She touched her lolly thoughtfully with the tip of her tongue. 'Tell you what, we can use the Domestipod shower instead.'

It wasn't a perfect solution, but it would have to do. Then they had to set the date and that proved tricky, not because of Uncle Bixbite's schedule, but because of Opal's.

'Not sure which night I can do,' she said. 'I have rather a lot of commitments, you know.'

'Commitments?' said Martha. Opal had only just

arrived. What kind of commitments could she possibly have?

'I've joined one or two after-school clubs, that's all.'

'OK,' said Martha. 'We'll work around them. Which days are you busy?'

Opal started checking the clubs off on the fingers of one hand. 'Monday's art club, Tuesday's hockey club, Wednesday's chess club, Thursday's netball club, Friday's fun club . . .' She looked at her hand, surprised to find she had run out of fingers on which to count.

'You're booked up every single day?' Martha had thought that the time after school would be special, reserved for her and Robbie.

'I wanted to do what the other school pupils were doing,' said Opal. 'That's what Uncle Bixie told me to do. And all the clubs sounded so tempting.'

Martha should have guessed Opal wouldn't be able to resist joining everything. 'All right,' she said with a sigh. 'What about *after* after-school clubs?'

Opal frowned. 'Well, I can't do Monday because I've been invited round to Lauren and Lisa's house. Tuesday, I'm going to Ravi's. Wednesday is Kayleigh's and Thursday's Colette's. Friday—'

'*Colette's!*' Martha burst out. 'You're going to *Colette's? For tea?*'

'Yes,' said Opal. 'She invited me. I didn't think it would be polite to say no. Should I have said no?'

'Yes,' said Martha firmly. Then, just as firmly, she said, 'No!' and then, raising her eyes to the sky, 'Oh, I don't know!'

Opal looked baffled.

'Somebody's jealous,' said Robbie, sticking his lolly in

his mouth so that he could scratch his head with both hands.

'I am not jealous,' Martha protested. 'It's not jealousy at all." Colette wasn't her enemy any more but it did feel peculiar, Opal planning tea dates with her.

'What's *jealousy*?' asked Opal, getting out her notebook and writing the word down. 'Sounds nice, like some sort of pudding.'

Martha shrugged with annoyance. Why couldn't Opal ever stick to the point? 'Look it up in your dictionary if you want to know.'

'Dokey hokey,' said Opal. 'I will.' She fluttered her eyelids, flicking through the dictionary in her brain until she came to the word she was looking for. '*Jealousy: A 'feeling of resentment towards a rival or competitor. Oh,*' she said, 'I didn't know you had a rival or a competitor, Martha. Do you?'

'No!' spluttered Martha. It wasn't just the tea with Colette that Martha was upset about, it was the fact Opal had arranged so many teas with so many different people. *She* was supposed to be Opal's Best and Only Friend. How come all these other people were involved now?

'They're only tea appointments, Martha,' said Opal. 'And you don't have to worry. You'll always be my Best and Only. I'm just behaving the way human beings are supposed to and having after school playful dates. I'm doing what Uncle Bixie says I have to do, so it's not worth getting your knickers in a twizzle, now is it?'

'My knickers are not in a twizzle,' Martha stood up on the pipe and waved her lollipop around crossly. 'My knickers are not even in a twist. You can have tea with anybody you like, Opal, it's a free country. All I'm asking you to do is find a time when Mrs Underedge can talk to Uncle Bixbite, so we can make her believe you're not living on your own, even though you are. So you can keep on going to school. So you can pass your CIA and not get sent to Drabbar. So you don't get taken into care. So you can keep Garnet with you. So you don't fade away to absolutely nothing at all until you actually stop breathing and DIE!'

Martha hadn't known she was going to make such a big speech. She stood panting slightly, trying to catch her breath.

No one said anything for a while. Opal and Robbie looked at Martha, and Martha looked back at them. Then, despite herself, she laughed. They both had such serious expressions on their faces but they also had brightly coloured lips, like clowns. Opal's were red from the outside of her lolly, and Robbie's were green from the inside of his.

'You do look silly,' Martha said, giggling.

Opal laughed too. She seemed relieved to have the opportunity. Opal didn't like awkward moments. 'You're very wise, Martha,' she said. 'You're as wise as a wise old robin. I should always listen to you. I'd be a nincompooper not to.'

'So you'll make the appointment?'

'I will,' said Opal. 'Next Thursday it is. I'll postpone Colette and I'll contact Uncle Bixie ASAS. Are you happier now, Best and Only?'

'Much happier.' She was too. She felt better for getting things off her chest and she was reassured that even though Opal was making new friends, it was only to fulfil her challenge. She and Robbie were Opal's true friends, the ones who really knew her, and Martha was still Opal's Best and Only.

Opal jumped up. 'And by the by-way, Martha,' she said. 'You look pretty silly yourself. You've got clown's lips too. Yellow ones.'

'Hey,' said Robbie, leaping to his feet. 'That's a full set of traffic lights. Let's be the traffic-light goons. We can have our own special signature moves. I'm the green goon and I go . . .' He did a crazy dance on top of the pipe.

Opal popped Garnet on her head and clapped her hands together. 'Ooh, lovely, a spanking new game! I'm the red goon and I go . . .' She did an even crazier dance.

'And I'm the amber goon,' said Martha. 'I go like this!' She pirouetted into the air, waving her lolly stick over her head.

'Follow me, goons,' said Robbie. 'By the left, qu-ick march!' He led Martha and Opal up and down the pipe, and they all practised their moves. It was a fun game, made even better by Opal who blinked her eyes and surrounded each of them in an aura of coloured light that matched the shade of their traffic light.

'Hold it!' Robbie stopped suddenly. 'Put the lights out quick!' He dropped to his knees and scrambled back between Martha and Opal's legs. The red, amber and green lights dropped away from them and flew into the pipe and out of sight. Robbie stayed where he was, with his head down.

'What's up with you?' said Martha.

'Creep alert!' he said. 'I've just seen Perry in the park. He's looking this way. You'll have to hide me.'

'Who's Perry?' said Opal.

'The new boy in Robbie's class,' said Martha. 'You must have seen him. Turns out he's quite keen on Robbie.'

'Keen?' said Robbie. 'He won't leave me alone. Follows me everywhere, keeps asking to be my friend. I can't get away from him. Not even in the toilets. I lock myself in but he looks under the door and goes all whiny. *Will you be my friend, Robbie, when you come out? Will you be my friendy-wendy?* He's such a creep!'

Martha could see Perry standing in the middle of the flower bed where the last of the flowers were still in bloom. He was with the woman she had seen going into Miss Brocklebank's office. They were both holding binoculars which they were pointing in the direction of the play area. Martha must have guessed correctly about the woman being Perry's mother. It was obvious really, since they looked so alike and both had their hair covered all the time. She gave them a wave. Immediately they turned away and began pointing their binoculars at the flowers instead.

'Where is he, then?' said Opal, scanning the park. 'Where is this creep? I want to know what one looks like.'

'He's not just a creep,' said Robbie from beneath the girls' legs. 'He's a super-creep. No, he's a mega-creep!'

'Over there, look,' said Martha. 'He's got his face in a flower. Can't you see?' Opal was usually the first to see everything. Not only could she see through things but she could also see a very long way, as far as France she claimed. So it was odd that she hadn't caught sight of Perry when he was only about fifty metres away.

Garnet could see him all right. He was barking and yip-yipping at him, like a tiny guard dog. Martha put out a hand to calm him and he whined and licked her fingers. 'Are your eyes all right, Opal?' she said. 'Have you got enough eyewash and cucumber slices for them?' Opal had to take great care of her eyes. They were the source of all her power.

Opal looked a little shifty. 'Oh yes,' she said. 'I've got plenty of that stuff. Don't worry. Anyway,' she added with a squint, 'I see him now. Pretty ordinary type of human, isn't he? Bit on the small side. I can see the flower very clearly. It's a pinky-orange one. I can see the name tag too. It's a dahlia, apparently, called Mango Bacon Spangle Surprise.'

'Never mind about the zooming dahlia,' said Robbie. 'Is he coming this way?'

'No,' said Martha. 'It's OK, they're going.' Perry and the woman were putting away their binoculars and walking hurriedly towards the gate at the opposite end of the park.

'Phewee!' Robbie scratched his head. 'I can't stand that Perry. I don't know how to get rid of him,' he said. 'He's way more irritating than head lice. And I've got to be in the cow suit with him, in *Jack and the Beanstalk*. Mr Morris said I needed someone to be Buttercup with me and Perry put his hand up, and now I'm stuck with him. I'm not letting him be the front end though. He stinks. He can go in the back. But I'm still going to need a gas mask. And when I come out I'll have to be blasted with extra-strong air freshener.'

'At least you've got a part in the play,' said Opal. 'I'm not even allowed to be in it.'

Opal was in Mrs Underedge's good books now. Ever since the teacher had cried in front of them and talked about little Letty, she had been much nicer to her. She had been nicer to everyone else too, all except Martha, who she still blamed for sneaking a look in her handbag. She had changed her mind about Garnet and allowed him to come into school each day; she had even made him his own special sleeping place, in a shopping basket, right by her desk. That was a relief. As long as Garnet didn't take it into his head to open his wings, he was one worry Martha could cross off her list.

There was one thing Mrs Underedge wouldn't do, though. She wouldn't go back on her decision not to give Opal a part in the play. Martha thought it was because she couldn't trust Opal not to start taking over the whole show. It would be just like her to do that.

'She'll come round,' said Opal, reading Martha's thoughts. 'I'll find a way to persuade her. By nook or by cook, I'll be on that stage with the rest of you, Best and Only. You wait and see!'

Chapter Thirteen

Martha saw surprisingly little of Opal over the next week. Even though they sat next to each other at school, there never seemed to be an opportunity to talk properly. Opal was so popular, she was always swept away from Martha at breaks, and there was a long line of people wanting to sit with her during lunch. After school she had her clubs and her play dates to go to.

Martha knew she would be able to spend time with Opal at the weekend, but it was still difficult, having to share her so much. Most days she hardly caught a glimpse of her after school had finished and it was often nearly bedtime when, watching from her window, Martha saw Opal finally going home to the Domestipod.

While Opal concentrated on her new social life, Martha kept herself busy making plans for the day when Mrs Underedge would visit the Domestipod. She wanted to make it look as much like a normal family home as possible. When Thursday came at last, Opal appeared straight after netball club as she had promised and the two of them went into the Domestipod to make

the final preparations. Robbie would have come too but his nits had got so bad that Mum had finally pinned him down in one of the hairdressing chairs at the salon and was giving him the Big T. He had tried to wriggle out of it by telling Mum his head would freeze off if she shaved all his hair. But Mum said he should have thought of that before he'd collected enough nits to fill Wembley football stadium, and that he would be fine if he wore a hat.

As Martha and Opal worked, Garnet flew around over their heads, stretching his wings. They needed stretching because he had to keep them folded away all day at school. Under Martha's direction, Opal cast her eyes around the room, bringing out the beanbag seats and the fridge, the tabletop and the two hammocks.

The trouble was, there was still nothing to indicate that there was anyone else living in the Domestipod apart from Opal and Garnet, and nothing at all belonging to a grown-up. Martha had brought some things to help with that. She had a big padded jacket of Mum's that could pass for a man's, which she slung over a chair, a packet of extra-spicy peanuts, a few of which she scattered on the tabletop, and best of all, a bottle of aftershave lotion she had bought at the mini-market where it had been on special offer. She sprinkled the strong-smelling liquid around the room while Opal looked on admiringly. 'Good work, Best and Only,' she said.

Martha was pleased Opal could see how much she had thought about the occasion. Opal didn't seem to notice her much at the moment. 'Now, three plates and ketchup,' she said. Opal produced both and Martha smeared some ketchup on the plates. She was just arranging knives and forks on top to make it look as if three people had recently finished a good meal when there was a knock on the door. Trust Mrs Underedge to be early. Martha looked at Opal. It was all down to her now. Where was Uncle Bixbite? Would he be there in time?

Opal winked at her and glanced at the door to open it. 'He'll be here,' she said. 'Don't worry, Martha. This plan is completely watery-tight.'

'Opal, dear,' said Mrs Underedge, stepping inside. 'What an unusual little bungalow!' She looked around curiously and breathed in the smell of aftershave. 'It's quite charming! Now, where is your uncle? Is he ready for me?'

'Almost, Mrs U,' said Opal. 'He's just had his tea with Martha and me.' She pointed extravagantly at the dirty plates. 'He's in a bit of a scurry though so he said he'd have to see you in his anniversary suit. Hope you don't mind.'

'Anniversary suit?' Mrs Underedge began. 'What's an—'

Her words were drowned out by a hissing and a rushing and a hundred violins all striking up at once. She stood back in alarm as Opal's shower cubicle came trundling out into the room. Inside it, half hidden by the painted clouds on the walls of the cubicle, and by the real clouds of steam that puffed around him, stood Uncle Bixbite. He wasn't all there. Most of him was on Carnelia. This was just the front of him, appearing on the hydrophone, a sort of heat and water-powered Carnelian videophone. He had taken off his shirt to assist with the illusion that he was really in the shower, washing to music.

Mrs Underedge gave a yelp and buried her face in her hands.

'Apologies for the birthday suit, dear lady,' said Uncle Bixbite. 'But I'm afraid I have a very tight schedule. I hope you don't mind.'

Mrs Underedge peeped at him through her fingers, like someone watching a scary but quite exciting TV programme. 'N-not at all,' she stammered. 'And I'm so sorry to interrupt your evening. I just wanted to make sure that Opal was all right and I see now that she's being very well looked after.' She gestured to the room Martha had arranged so carefully.

'Naturally,' said Uncle Bixbite, 'Opal is my top priority. And yours too, I trust. How is she doing at school?'

'Oh, I'm having a shark of a time, at school,' Opal butted in. 'It's far off! The only thing is,' she said, rather slyly Martha thought, 'I haven't got a part in the school play. I haven't even got one measly-mumpy line!'

'Do all the other children have parts?' enquired Uncle Bixbite. 'Do they all have lines?'

'Yes, Uncle,' said Opal, pouting. 'Every child in Merry Class has a role to play, apart from me.'

Uncle Bixbite frowned through the steam. 'You know the rules, Opal,' he said sternly. 'You must be the same as everyone else. It's vital.' He turned to Mrs Underedge and boomed, 'Why is there no part for my Opal, dear lady?' His voice echoed around the room. *Dear lady, dear lady, lady . . .*

Mrs Underedge's cheeks, which were already quite pink, went three shades pinker. 'Oh,' she said, 'well . . .

that is . . . as a matter of fact . . . I've been thinking and there is a part for Opal. Of course there is. She's going to be the . . . the beanstalk!'

'Oh, fabtickytastic!' said Opal, with a whoop. 'The title role! Now that's what I call a result!'

'Excellent,' said Uncle Bixbite, beginning to soap his armpit. 'Then everything is as it should be. I'm glad that's settled.'

Seeing Uncle Bixbite actually washing in front of her was far too much for Mrs Underedge. Her face was now a vivid beetroot red. 'Good gracious!' she said. 'Is that the time? I really must be going. Lovely to meet you, Mr Biscuit . . . I mean Bixbite . . . I mean Uncle . . . Captain . . . Moonbaby. And thank you for all you're doing on the space shuttle or . . . space station or . . . or . . .' Her voice trailed away.

'Goodbye.' Uncle Bixbite nodded regally and Mrs Underedge backed out of the door, bowing, like someone who had just been dismissed by the Queen. Uncle Bixbite always had that effect on people. Martha remembered trembling a little when Opal had first introduced her to him. Very slowly, she knelt down behind Opal's beanbags, hoping he wouldn't look her way now.

'Thanks a trillion, Uncle Bixie,' said Opal, as the door closed. 'Good of you to pop up and help out.'

Martha thought the shower cubicle and Opal's uncle might go back to their rightful places then but they didn't. The water continued to pour down, music continued to play and steam continued to billow around the paper-thin image of Uncle Bixbite.

'Now that you've disturbed me, Opal,' he said, 'I may

as well check on your progress. Are you keeping a low profile this time, as I instructed?'

'Lower than low,' said Opal in a deep voice.

'Low' was not how Martha would have described Opal's profile. But she wasn't about to contradict her in front of Uncle Bixbite.

'And the Human Handybook?'

'Oh, that's as good as done.' Opal took out her tiny notebook and flapped it in the air. 'It was easy-peasy-lemon-squishy.'

'Good. Then it sounds as if you are well on the way to earning your Carnelian Independence Award at last.' Uncle Bixbite's mingle – part bat, part bird – flew up and hung from his chin like a beard. Uncle Bixbite stroked the upside-down creature thoughtfully. 'And what of the Mercurials? Have you had any sightings of them?'

The Mercurials. Martha had forgotten about them. Hearing the name of the most unpleasant clan on Carnelia gave her an odd feeling, like a jigsaw piece was slotting itself into some big puzzle in her mind. The trouble was that the jigsaw puzzle in her mind didn't have a lid, or a picture to follow, so she wasn't sure what it was a puzzle *of* exactly.

Opal snorted. 'No sightings at all! There can't be a Mercurial for kilometres around. If there was, I would have seen them. I would have seen them off too, and no mistake.'

'Nevertheless,' warned Uncle Bixbite, 'I urge you to be cautious. There are a great many rumblings on Carnelia at present. Rumour has it that the Mercurials have sent a deputation to Earth to find you. They will sabotage your progress if they can, Opal. Then they may try to prove that they are worthy claimants to the Carnelian Coronet. As worthy as the Moonbabies.'

'Worthy!' scoffed Opal. 'Don't make me laugh out loud. A Mercurial has about as much worth as a duck pimple.'

'A Mercurial has about as much worth as a *goose* pimple,' corrected her uncle. 'And be that as it may,' he went on, 'the Mercurials could be here already. They may be on this planet, trying to do as you did, Opal. They may be trying to befriend an Earth child at this very minute, just as you befriended young Martha here.' Martha hadn't realised he had seen her, tucked among the beanbags. She stood up at once and curtsied to him.

Opal laughed. 'The Mercurials will never manage that,' she cackled. 'Human beings are far too sensible to make friends with Mercurials.'

'Don't be so sure. Mercurials are devious demons. They may be unsavoury creatures who can see no further than the ends of their own little noses but their hair is powerful. You should never underestimate the power of Mercurial hair.'

'Power to do what?' Opal said. 'To be curly or straight? Or put into bunches, or a horsey-tail? Or maybe a bun? With a cherry on top? Ooh, I'm really scared!' She put her fingers to her mouth and began to tiptoe quickly around the room, pretending she was being chased by a Mercurial.

'Stop!' Uncle Bixbite's voice filled the Domestipod with its resonance. At the sound of it, his mingle's eagle eyes snapped open, glassy and golden. Opal stood still at last as Uncle Bixbite and the mingle fixed her with matching stares.

'The Mercurials can do more than that, Opal. Much more. If a Moonbaby is covered from head to toe in Mercurial hair, they lose their eye power forever. If a Moonbaby loses their power they are stripped of all rights to live on Carnelia. If you should be covered with Mercurial hair while you are on Earth, you will never inherit the Carnelian Coronet. You will not even be able to return home. You will be sent to live out your remaining years alone on Drabbar, the most barren planet in the universe. That is the Carnelian Law. Life on Drabbar is a fate I would not wish on anyone, Opal, but if the Mercurials cover you with their hair, your future will no longer be in my control.'

Martha's ears tingled at the mention of Drabbar. So it really did exist. She had half wondered if Opal had made it up to impress her but now she was in no doubt. She believed everything Uncle Bixbite said and she was greatly disturbed by his speech.

Opal wasn't disturbed. She caught Garnet as he flew by her on the way to his hammock and started stroking him. 'How are they going to do that then?' she said. 'Cover me up in their hair without me noticing? I'd see that hair coming and light-laser it to Jupiter with one wink!'

Uncle Bixbite shook his head. 'You are young, Opal, and you believe yourself invincible. Yet you are vulnerable here on Earth. You must be on your guard at all times. Are you taking proper care of your eyes?'

'Of course,' said Opal. 'Look.' She glanced at a wall and

117

a rack of cucumbers, eyewash and eye packs appeared. 'The mini-market's ordering boxes of this stuff for me every week.'

Uncle Bixbite seemed reassured. 'Good. And have you been back to Muckle Flugga for a recharge yet? Your eye power must be kept at its absolute maximum in case of an emergency; that's more important now than ever. I trust there have been no unnecessary tricks? No coloured light effects or fancy stars? You know how draining such antics can be.'

'Oh no,' said Opal, making her eyes look all round and innocent. 'No antics at all.'

Garnet opened his mouth and said, *'Yip-yi-yi,'* but Opal clamped her fingers around his muzzle. Martha looked down at the floor. She was thinking of the string of violet stars Opal had encircled them with on that first day in the Domestipod, and the traffic-light auras she had produced when they were playing on the pipe.

Uncle Bixbite sighed as if he knew perfectly well Opal wasn't telling the truth. His mingle fluttered restlessly against his neck.

'I will not be able to help you any further. I have many duties to perform. The responsibility of the Carnelian Coronet is a weighty one and I must return my full attention to Matters of Planet. Meanwhile, I will leave you with a list of names of all Mercurials currently absent from Carnelia.'

He tossed something out of the top of the cubicle and Opal caught it. It was a damp towel, covered with strange white writing.

'Many of these Mercurials are, no doubt, roaming

118

space, looking for trouble in other solar systems, but some of them may be here on Earth. They will be looking for you, Opal. They are closer than you think. Be aware and be wary!'

He turned to Martha. His voice was fading but she heard him say, 'Take care of her, child.'

'I will. I promise,' she told his watery image as it started to ripple and break up and disappear.

Then the water stopped showering, the steam subsided and the musical accompaniment began to fade away. The now empty shower cubicle rolled back into its place in the wall.

'Mission complete,' said Opal with a toss of her head. She balled up the towel and shoved it in a laundry box which followed the shower cubicle into some hidden recess in the Domestipod wall.

Martha was amazed. 'Aren't you even going to look at it?' she said.

Opal laughed. 'Oh, Best and Only,' she said, 'Do stop panicking. The Mercurials aren't coming to Archwell. They wouldn't dare!'

'But what if you're wrong? What if they did dare?'

'Well, if they did dare, you silly sausage roll,' Opal answered, 'I'd know, wouldn't I? I do have Z-ray vision, don't forget!'

'X-ray,' corrected Martha.

'No,' said Opal. 'It's Z-ray and that's about a zillion times stronger than your Earth X-rays, so you can stop worrying.'

Martha wanted to quiz Opal some more about the tricks she had seen her do with her eyes. She wanted to know how and when she was supposed to go to the lighthouse on Muckle Flugga for the recharge. Opal hadn't mentioned anything about that. But before Martha could say anything else, Opal cried, 'Robbie alert!' She nodded at the door. It opened and Robbie burst in.

'Has he come yet?' he panted. 'Did I miss anything?'

Chapter Fourteen

'Sorry,' said Martha. 'Uncle Bixbite left a minute ago.'

'Oh, great!' Robbie threw himself on a beanbag next to Garnet. 'I've been stuck in the salon listening to Alesha whinging on about how she can't get hold of any Luxury Locks hair conditioner, while you've been here talking to the King of Carnelia! It's so unfair.' He lifted his head. 'What was it like anyway? Was it awesome?'

'It was,' said Opal, bounding onto the table with glee. 'And there's great news, Robbie. Thanks to Uncle Bixie, I've got a part in the school play at last. I'm going to be the beanstalk. The actual beanstalk!' She bounced excitedly, making the tongue-shaped tabletop spring up and down like a diving board. 'I'm so excited. I'm over the stars. I'm going to be the beanstalk, the beanstalk!'

'I don't know why you're so happy about it,' said Robbie glumly. 'The beanstalk gets chopped down in the end.'

Opal bounced off the table and plopped down next to him. 'What's the matter, Cucumber Hero? Is it because you've had all your hair cut off?' She stroked the remaining nit-and-lice-free stubble on Robbie's head. If Martha had tried to do that, Robbie would have shaken

her off immediately but he didn't seem to mind Opal doing it.

'It's not the Big T,' he said. 'I don't care about that. I don't even care that Alesha made me wipe down the chair and disinfect all her combs after I'd had it done.'

'What is it then?' said Martha.

Robbie groaned. 'It's Perry!'

'What about him?'

'He's found me.'

'Found you, Cucumber Hero?' said Opal. 'I didn't know you were lost.'

'No,' said Robbie. 'I'm not. I mean he's found out where I live, where Mum works and everything. He and his aunt, they came into the salon while I was having the Big T and they asked me over to their place, to play with Perry!'

'You didn't say you'd go, did you?' said Martha.

'*I* didn't. Mum did.'

'Why?'

'I don't know. I tried to stop her. I made a load of faces at her in the mirror but she didn't even notice. She just kept cutting my hair and being all polite and sort of sing-songy, *"Oh yes, Robbie would love to come, wouldn't you, Robbie?"* Mum can be so annoying sometimes.'

'But didn't you explain to her?' said Martha. 'After they'd gone I mean.'

'Course I did,' said Robbie. 'But she said it would be rude to change the arrangement now. Which is totally unfair since I wasn't the one who did any arranging in the first place.'

'So you've got to go?'

Robbie grunted. 'Yes. Only once though. Mum said

if I didn't like it I'd never have to go again.'

'There you are,' said Opal, jumping up and starting to juggle the cutlery from the table. 'Every cloud has a silver stuffing!'

'Silver lining, you mean,' said Robbie. 'Actually, that reminds me.' He gave a small smile and slowly pulled something from his pocket. 'There is one good thing.'

'What's that?' said Martha looking at the small box he was holding. 'Did Mum give you chocolate raisins?' She usually gave him some sort of treat after he'd had the Big T.

'Now,' said Robbie, putting on his mysterious magician's face and giving the box a slight shake. 'You may think this looks like an ordinary box of chocolate raisins, but it isn't.'

Opal stopped juggling and looked at the box, seeing through its sides. 'So it isn't!' she exclaimed. 'Whatever are you doing with those things?'

'I'm keeping them,' said Robbie. 'As pets.'

'What are they?' said Martha. The box didn't look big enough for even one tiny mouse. 'What have you got in there, Robbie?'

'They're my head lice. I rescued a few before Mum could get me with the clippers. I've got three. I'm keeping them in here. It's a head lice animal sanctuary. I pulled out some hair and put it in with them so they'll feel at home.'

'And you're feeding them with your own blood, I notice,' said Opal, who could see more of what was going on in the closed box than Martha even wanted to see.

'Yep,' said Robbie proudly. 'I grated my finger with the cheese grater so I could give them some blood to eat. It hurt like crazy but I'm going to do it every day from now on.' He opened the box a crack and peeped in. 'All right, boys?' he said.

'That's disgusting,' said Martha. 'Mum's going to kill you when she finds out.'

'I know,' said Robbie. 'But she's not going to find out. You have to promise never to tell her about Mark and Kevin and Clive. All right?'

Martha shrugged. 'All right.'

Opal was flicking open her notebook and adding a few notes.

'This Human Handybook is going terrifyingly well. Can I read it to you?'

She didn't wait for an answer but riffled quickly through the tiny pages, reading aloud. '"Human beings! Human beings like cheesy puffs, chocolate raisins and nose picking and tickling. They have tears that come out of their eyes for reasons or sometimes no reason at all. They also have TV, football, pirates and jealousy." I've put in brackets, "this is not a pudding". Then it goes, "They like to keep pets, such as cats, like little Letty, and head lice, like Mark and Kevin and Clive."' Opal wrote in the last few words and then drew a very bold full stop. She looked up. 'What do you think?'

'Yup,' said Robbie, 'You've pretty well covered it. Don't you think so, Martha?'

'We-ell . . .' Martha began.

'That's lucky,' said Opal, giving the little book a shake, 'because I've almost run out of pages. It's a good thing you humans don't lead complicated lives!'

Chapter Fifteen

Life *was* complicated, though, for Martha at least. At school the next week, she tried harder than ever to keep Opal out of trouble. Uncle Bixbite's warning about the Mercurials and the terrible-sounding planet Drabbar ran round and round in her head and she was determined to take her promise to him to look after Opal very seriously. But looking after an alien wasn't easy, and the more Martha tried to take care of Opal, the more trouble she seemed to get into herself.

When they were doing cooking and Opal didn't have an apron, Martha lent Opal hers, and then got told off for not wearing an apron herself. If Opal wasn't listening to what Mrs Underedge was telling them, Martha whispered things to her, and was then punished for talking in class. She spent so long making sure that Opal did her homework and brought it into school on time that she forgot to bring in her own homework three days running, and Mrs Underedge put her on litter duty for a week. It wasn't Opal's name that kept appearing on the board now. It was Martha's. It wasn't Opal who kept being sent out to

spend time looking at the coat pegs and lockers, it was Martha.

Opal was having a great time. She and Mrs Underedge were getting on brilliantly now. After her visit to the Domestipod, Mrs Underedge was being even kinder to Opal. She kept asking her how her *space-travelling uncle* was doing, and whether he would be coming to see *Jack and the Beanstalk*. She always blushed when she said that. And she paid Opal lots of extra attention, especially when they were rehearsing for the play.

One day Mrs Underedge arrived in the school hall with a big bunch of bamboo canes from her garden. She spent half the morning building a special enclosure on the stage for Opal to stand in as the beanstalk. She put a set of steps inside the enclosure and, in order to show that the beanstalk was growing, Opal climbed slowly up the steps, hooking green shoots and leaves onto the bamboo canes as she went. Mrs Underedge had made the leaves out of green felt, left over from last year's production of *Robin Hood*. Opal had a costume now too, consisting of a long-sleeved green T-shirt and green leggings, with an orange runner-bean flower which she pinned to the top of her hair.

Opal didn't have any lines but she made lots of creaking and squeaking noises which were supposed to be the sound of the beanstalk growing and swaying in the breeze. She made these noises nearly all the time, regardless of who else was speaking. No one seemed to mind because it was so funny.

Martha was kneeling on a big table at the back of the stage. She had a wooden framework harnessed to her back. It was her harp costume and it was lined with cardboard tubes of different lengths, taken from the insides of rolls of cling film and kitchen foil. These were meant to be her harp strings and they were going to be sprayed with gold paint in time for the performance. She had to sit on the table for ages, waiting for the moment when she was supposed to sing to the giant.

'You OK, Martha?' said Jessie. 'That thing looks really uncomfortable.' Jessie was standing behind the table, wearing a frilly apron and rolling out pretend pastry for the giant's dinner.

'I'm fine,' said Martha, shifting around on her knees. 'My legs have gone to sleep, that's all.'

Jessie waved her rolling pin at Martha's legs. 'Wake up, you lazy limbs!' she said and tutted in the shrill voice she used when she was being the giant's wife.

Martha smiled. She had got to know Jessie much better since rehearsals began. They'd spent ages together waiting to practise their scene and had become quite skilled at holding whispered conversations, just quiet enough not to attract Mrs Underedge's attention.

'Watch out,' Jessie whispered now. 'She's looking our way.' She went back to her rolling.

'Castle kitchen scene next,' said Mrs Underedge. 'Be ready, giant's wife, giant's harp and giant's rabbit. Listen for your cue, it's, "I'll grind his bones to make my bread."'

Martha stroked Garnet who was sitting next to her on the table. He had a part in the play too. Mrs Underedge had cast him as the giant's rabbit and given him some extra long ears which he wore over his own lynx ones. It was silly really. Garnet was already a mix of six different animals and now he had been given a seventh.

Opal was so happy, standing there in her bamboo cane enclosure, right in the middle of the stage, just where she'd always wanted to be. Martha didn't admit it but deep down *she* wasn't feeling very happy. Nothing had turned out the way she had imagined it would. She had thought being Opal's Best and Only Friend meant just that. But Opal had about a million best friends and Martha barely saw her. She was even best friends with Mrs Underedge. They were deep in conversation now, discussing the beanstalk's characteristics. Watching them like that gave Martha an odd sensation. She felt as if she were looking at a display in a shop window. Mrs Underedge and Opal and all the other children on the stage were part of the display, but she wasn't.

There was a long silence. Martha realised she had drifted off into her thoughts, and missed her cue after all. Everyone was looking at her.

'Martha!' screeched Mrs Underedge. 'Will the harp be singing for us this side of Christmas or must we wait until ... *Whitsuntide?*'

'Sorry.' Martha cleared her throat and began to sing very quietly. Her song had a lovely lilting tune and she already knew it off by heart.

'No need to be sad, Sir,
No need for you to frown.
No need to be down, Sir,
Not when I'm around.
I will sing to you, Sir,
Lift your heart up high.
I will sing to you, Sir,
Raise your spirits to the sky.'

'Hmm,' said Mrs Underedge. 'Well, at least you know the words. But sing up, Martha, will you? And do try to smile. Be joyful. You'll have the poor giant weeping into his golden poached eggs if you do it like that.'

Martha tried to sound happier but she couldn't help it. The tune was just so beautiful and whenever she sang it, she felt a strange kind of wishing and yearning which left her feeling really sad.

She thought Opal might notice the sadness and ask her about it, but she didn't. For someone with the ability to read minds, Opal could be surprisingly insensitive. Martha supposed that Opal only read people's thoughts when it suited her to do so. If she wasn't interested in what you were thinking she simply didn't look. In the summer Martha had had to tell Opal to stop reading her thoughts all the time. Now she would have liked it if she had read them a bit more often. She told herself that Opal would calm down eventually, once she was used to school and her new way of life. After all, there was still a whole ten months before Opal was due to go back to Carnelia. It was just a matter of being patient. Soon they could get on with being Best and Only Friends again. Martha was almost sure of it.

☆ ☆ ☆

Martha walked home by herself that evening. Opal was doing art club and then going to Lauren and Lisa's house for tea. She didn't forget about Martha completely. She came rushing up to her after the bell went and said, 'There's a spare place in art club, Martha. Why don't you come along? We could do a joint picture.'

Martha was about to answer when Lauren and Lisa swooped in. 'Come on, Opal,' said Lisa. 'You're sitting with us today!'

'Yes,' said Lauren. 'We're going to do your portrait!'

'Coming?' said Opal, as the twins started to pull her towards the art room.

'No,' said Martha. 'No, thanks. Actually I said I'd help Mum cook the tea.' She could tell there'd be no chance to talk to Opal, so what was the point?

'See you tomorrow then, Best and Only,' said Opal. 'I'm off to paint a masterbit!'

'*Masterpiece*, you mean!' squealed Lauren and Lisa in unison, as they whisked Opal away.

Robbie had already gone off with Perry and the funny little woman that Martha now knew was his aunt. They had looked really pleased about the play date. They had each taken one of Robbie's hands in their own little pudgy ones and led him proudly out of school, as if he was some sort of trophy. There was something very odd about the way they had put their faces right up to Robbie's. They seemed to be sniffing him. Martha guessed they were doing it because they were so short-sighted. Maybe they didn't realise how close they were getting.

Robbie had gazed back at Martha mournfully, cringing like a condemned pirate starting his final walk down the gangplank.

He didn't come home for ages. Martha felt quite sorry for him. She was sitting in their bedroom looking out at the empty Domestipod when he finally came in. He went straight over to the bunks and retrieved the raisin box from under his pillow.

'How was it?' said Martha sympathetically.

'Fantastic!' said Robbie, opening the box and checking on Mark and Kevin and Clive. 'I had the best time ever.'

'What?' said Martha. 'You are joking?'

'No, it was ace. It was one of the best play dates I've ever had.'

Martha was amazed. 'But you hate Perry. You said you wouldn't touch him with a telescope, not even an extra-extendible one. You can't stand being next to him. You said he smells.'

Robbie shrugged. 'The smell's not so bad, not once you get used to it. He's quite funny actually, and clever. And his auntie's really nice too. She says I can call her Auntie Minnie if I want.' He fingered something on his arm. At first Martha thought it was a big hairy spider that he was flicking off his skin, but when she looked closer she saw that whatever it was was attached to Robbie and knotted securely around his wrist.

'What's that on your arm?'

'Oh, nothing,' said Robbie casually, pulling down his sleeve.

'Are you wearing a bracelet?'

'Only a small one.' Robbie looked embarrassed. 'It's not really a bracelet anyway. It's more of a friendship band.'

'From Zack?' said Martha. It wasn't like Robbie to wear a bracelet. He said jewellery was for girls, but she thought he might wear a bracelet, or a friendship band, if Zack had given it to him. 'Did he send it to you from Cornwall?'

'Oh no, it's not from Zack. It's from Perry.' Robbie touched the bracelet again, holding out his arm for

Martha to see. 'Auntie Minnie made it. She's a weaver apparently. She's got this amazing loom thing. They showed it to me. Perry says she weaves things like this all the time.'

The bracelet was made of black and brown strands of wool or maybe cotton. It looked thick and wiry, tough as a bootlace.

'Wicked, isn't it?' said Robbie. 'It's strong too. I tried to get it off on the way home but I couldn't undo the knot. It won't budge, not even with scissors. Perry doesn't want me to take it off though, so I may as well keep it on.'

Martha frowned in disbelief. Why was Robbie suddenly being so careful not to upset Perry? There was something very weird about all this.

'I'm going again tomorrow,' said Robbie. 'Perry's promised to show me his locust-grub.'

'What's a locust-grub?'

'Exactly,' said Robbie. 'I'd never heard of one either. But Perry's got one and I want to check it out. It's some kind of pet, I think. And Martha, you'll never guess where Perry lives. He and Auntie Minnie, they've got this incredible caravan thing, called a motorhome. They've parked it round the back of the bus depot. They travel about in it, go wherever they like.' He threw himself down on his bed. 'They said they might even take me one day. I could go on holiday with them. On safari to Africa or Scotland or Bognor Regis. How cool would that be?!'

'Hang on a minute,' said Martha. 'You said Perry was a mega-creep. And now you're planning to go on holiday with him. What's going on?' She could see how Robbie would like the motorhome and be intrigued by the locust-grub, or whatever Perry's pet was, but it didn't explain why he had changed his mind so quickly and so completely about Perry himself. He was still the same creepy, weird person. Martha couldn't understand it.

'I wasn't going to be friends with Perry,' said Robbie. 'But that was before I knew him properly. Mum's right, you shouldn't judge a book by its cover. You should definitely wait until you've read the first page.' He tucked in the flap on the raisin box and stuck it in his pocket. 'Now if you've finished asking me questions, Mark and Kevin and Clive and me are off to brush our teeth.'

Martha stood at the window listening to the bathroom tap running on full, while Robbie brushed and gargled noisily. She felt stunned. This was an amazing turnaround. It didn't make sense. For some reason, the thought of Robbie going back to Perry's again gave Martha a queasy feeling.

Then she forgot about Robbie for a moment because she could see Opal finally arriving back at the Domestipod. Lauren and Lisa and their mum were dropping her off. As the car pulled away Opal ran alongside it, waving madly at the two girls waving back at her from the passenger seats.

Martha felt a pang of sadness. She wished she was the one Opal was waving at. But no sooner had she made the wish than Opal looked up and blew a kiss in Martha's direction. She widened her eyes and followed the kiss with her gaze until it turned into a silver heart. Chased along by Opal's eyes, the heart floated up to Martha's window and touched the glass for a moment before dissolving into the night.

Martha felt better immediately. She knew Opal wouldn't be sending hearts and things to Lauren and Lisa and the rest of them. Nevertheless she put up a finger in warning. Opal was supposed to be saving her eye power for important occasions. Opal wasn't looking any more though. She was already going inside and the Domestipod was glowing its warm glow. Martha sighed. She would have to wait until the next day to give Opal a proper reminder.

Chapter Sixteen

Martha thought Robbie might have come to his senses by morning, but he hadn't. He talked non-stop about Perry all the way to school and as far as Martha could see, he spent the entire day with him. When she came out for break, he was sitting with Perry on the wall. Robbie never sat on the wall. He never sat still at all if he could help it. He always played football or ran around pretending to be a bloodthirsty pirate, chasing landlubbers with a cutlass. Now though, he just sat cross-legged next to Perry, talking and sniggering. Martha went by a couple of times with Jessie; she tried to listen in but Jessie was chatting and the boys dropped their voices to whispers when she passed so it was impossible to hear what they were saying. It was odd but Martha really felt the need to know what they were talking about. They didn't have a thing in common and yet whatever they were discussing was keeping them both completely engrossed. Martha must be missing something, but she couldn't think what.

Robbie didn't mind sharing the cow suit with Perry now. In fact, when they came in for rehearsal that

afternoon he could hardly wait to jump inside it and get zipped up in there with him. Martha noticed that he let Perry be the front end too, despite what he had said before about how he was going to make him be the back.

They were so involved in whatever they were doing in the cow suit that they didn't even notice when Mrs Underedge announced a break. Martha was relieved to take off her heavy harp costume and she was already on her way out of the hall, after Opal and the others, when she realised that Buttercup was still sitting on stage. She thought Robbie and Perry might be stuck so she went back and unzipped Buttercup's head.

The two boys were sitting squashed together in the haunches of the cow suit. They squinted up at her and Martha saw what was keeping them so occupied. Perry had brought his pet with him. His locust-grub. It was lying curled in Robbie's cupped palm. It was pale and fleshy, almost white, with several sets of legs and two pinhole eyes. It looked like a maggot to Martha, except maggots didn't have wings and this thing had two pairs of long ones. They were a bit like dragonflies' wings, only instead of being transparent they were spattered with muddy brown splodges.

'Hi, Martha,' said Robbie. 'Meet Beryl.' He held out his hand towards her. 'Cute, isn't she?'

Martha was pretty sure she had never seen anything less cute in her entire life. She took a step back as the creature writhed around in Robbie's palm. It was leaving a sticky goo all over his hand, like a snail trail, but Robbie didn't care. He seemed genuinely to like the creature. Martha thought it was revolting. 'She's very . . . unusual,' she said, trying not to grimace in disgust.

'She's not just unusual,' Perry lisped. 'She's unique. Beryl's the only locust-grub in the whole world. I'm letting Robbie hold her because he's my friendy-wendy, aren't you, Robbie-wobbie?' He plucked at the bracelet round Robbie's wrist and used it to hold up Robbie's hand, the one that wasn't holding Beryl.

'Yessy-wessy,' said Robbie, smiling as he allowed Perry to lift his arm in the air. 'I am.'

Martha couldn't believe her ears. How could Robbie, of all people, listen to this boy's baby talk without cringing? How could he join in with it?

'Will you take our photo-woto?' said Perry, retrieving a disposable camera from one of Buttercup's hind legs.

'No,' said Martha. 'You're not allowed to bring cameras to school.'

'Oh, go on,' wheedled Perry. 'It'll only take a secondy-wecondy.'

'Yes, go on, Martha,' said Robbie. 'Just take it. Don't be such a spoilsport.'

Perry wrapped his arm around Robbie, pressing his clammy-looking cheek against his face.

'Say cheesy-weesy!' said Perry.

'Cheesy-weesy!' said both boys. Martha clicked the button and hastily handed the camera back to Perry.

'Is my auntie-wauntie here yet?' he said, peering out of the cow costume into the hall. He didn't seem to be able to see very far at all, despite the strong lenses in his glasses.

'Your aunt?' said Martha. 'I don't think so. Why?'

'Auntie Minnie's coming to help with the play,' said Robbie. 'She's making something for it too, on her loom. I saw her weaving it last night. It's something for the backdrop. I don't know what it is yet, but it's going to be really big, isn't it, Perry?'

'Yes,' simpered Perry. 'It's going to be enormous-wormous.' The boys giggled as the doors opened at the back of the hall and people started to come back in for the next rehearsal session.

Perry took Beryl from Robbie and pushed her up into his hairnet. She squelched and clicked a bit and then she was out of sight. 'Looks like we missed the breakie-weakie,' Perry said. 'Never mind. Zip us back up will you, Robbie's sister, Martha.' Martha was only too happy to zip up the cow suit so that she couldn't see his sneering face any longer. As she pulled the zip closed, she felt the return of that inexplicable queasy feeling she had had when Robbie came home the previous night. She found herself thinking about that jigsaw puzzle again, the one that had come into her mind when Uncle Bixbite had visited, the one with no picture to follow. If she could just get a look at some more of the pieces she thought she would be able to figure something out. But what was it?

'Act Two,' called Mrs Underedge. 'Places everyone. Our adult helpers are coming in this afternoon. Let's see if we can impress them, shall we?'

Martha put on her harp costume again and kneeled on the giant's table. They were rehearsing the scene where Jack and his mother realise the beanstalk has grown as tall as their house in one night. Tom and Chloe were supposed to be gazing up in astonishment at the beanstalk, but Opal, on her stepladder, was pulling faces at them and their looks of astonishment kept turning into snorts and giggles. Martha didn't laugh. She had found Opal's messing around as funny as everyone else at first but now she was just longing for some more quiet time with her. She didn't feel properly close to Opal at the moment, not like a Best and Only Friend should feel. When would it ever be just the two of them?

A hissing sound behind her made Martha jump. She looked over her shoulder to see Perry's Auntie Minnie reaching up and spraying gold paint over her harp strings.

'Sorry, darling. Did I startlify you? Still as a statue now,' she went on, without giving Martha a chance to answer. 'Don't move a muscular. This won't take long.'

Martha faced the front again and tried to keep still. She tried not to breathe too. The smell of the spray paint, combined with the woman's sickly perfume, made her feel as if she was inhaling poison.

Perry's aunt stopped spraying at last and appeared in front of Martha. She was so short and the giant's table was so tall that she only came up to Martha's waist now. 'That ought to do it,' she said, blinking at Martha from behind her glasses, her traffic cone headwrap nodding slightly as she spoke.

'Thank you,' Martha said, trying not to breathe in. 'Thank you, Mrs . . .' Her voice trailed off. She didn't know what to call her.

'Call me Auntie Minnie,' said the woman, smiling and showing her blunt brown teeth.

Martha knew she would never be able to call this person 'Auntie'. She wasn't her idea of an auntie at all. Aunties were supposed to be warm and comforting people. Martha had never met anyone less like an auntie in her life.

'Make sure you don't move for the next ten minutes, all right, sugary-pie? While it dries.'

It wasn't really all right. Martha's knees were already hurting from kneeling down for so long. Now she would have to stay here even longer. She didn't know why Perry's aunt couldn't have asked her to take the harp off her back first. That would have been much more sensible.

'Now we can have a lovely little chat, can't we?' whispered Auntie Minnie, raising her bushy eyebrows, as though she and Martha shared some sort of secret. 'Just you and me.'

Just you and me! Martha couldn't think of anything worse. Perry's Auntie Minnie gave her the creeps. She was so peculiar, with her odd long robes and her orange headwrap. Martha found herself staring at the headwrap, looking for the green ribbon she had mistaken for a tail. There was nothing sticking out of the scarf this time but Martha fancied that she saw movement inside it, as if something was burrowing around inside.

'I've been watching you, Martha,' said Auntie Minnie. She was standing much too close and Martha could smell her sour breath.

'H-have you?' Martha stammered.

'Yes,' said Minnie with another of her horrible brown smiles. 'I've had my beady eye on you and I've been thinking to myself, "That Martha's lonely. She needs a little cheerying up; she needs a friend." So I've made something for you.'

Martha swallowed nervously. She hadn't told anyone she was feeling lonely, although she was. The idea that Minnie had had her beady eye on her gave her a spooky feeling, and not in a good way.

She watched as Minnie pulled something from her pocket. It looked very similar to the friendship band Perry had given to Robbie, only longer. It was made of black and orange strands, all closely woven together.

'It's a choker,' explained Auntie Minnie. 'I wove it myself. You wear it round your throat, nice and tight. Shall I put it on for you?' She began to reach around Martha's neck, her stubby fingers catching in Martha's hair.

'No!' Martha said suddenly, pushing away the woman's hands. If there was one thing she knew, it was that she didn't want this choker to be tied round her throat. She didn't know why she felt so strongly about it, but she did. The choker fell to the ground and they both stared at it as it lay on the stage in the dust.

'Quiet!' Mrs Underedge called, frowning in Martha's direction. 'We must have everyone's *absolute concentration*. The performance is only two weeks away. We are running out of time!'

'Oh, dearie me,' whispered Auntie Minnie. 'You've made me drop it.' She bent to pick up the choker. 'Not very grateful of you, is it?' Her eyes looked so hard for a moment. Then they seemed to soften a little as she widened them and said, 'Don't you want it then? My little treasured one?'

Martha didn't say that she had never wanted anything less, and that she was not and never would be Auntie Minnie's 'little treasured one'. That wouldn't have been polite. So she said, 'I'm sorry, but Mrs Underedge wouldn't like it. We're not allowed to wear jewellery in Merry Class.'

Auntie Minnie pursed her lips in barely disguised annoyance. 'I hadn't thought of that,' she said, giving Mrs Underedge what Martha thought was an unnecessarily fierce glare.

She turned to Martha again, switching back on her smile. 'Well, my poppety,' she said. 'You just let me know if you change your mind about my little gift-tag. It's yours whenever you want it.' She waved the choker under Martha's nose and then pocketed it. 'You're nearly dry now so I'll leave you to it.'

To Martha's relief, Auntie Minnie stalked away into the wings. She didn't leave the stage altogether though. She stopped, turned round and stared. Not at Martha, but at Opal. It was a horrible stare. She stared so hard at the back of Opal's head, as if she would like to bore a hole right through her skull. Why was she looking at Opal with such hatred?

Anyone else glancing at Auntie Minnie then might have thought she was just peering at Opal like that because she was so short-sighted. No one else had glasses as thick as the ones Perry and his aunt wore. But Martha was watching very closely and there was no mistaking that look; it was definitely filled with hate; so much so that Auntie Minnie's tiny nose was wrinkling and twitching with hatred too.

Martha shivered as she suddenly remembered something Uncle Bixbite had said about the Mercurials. They were unsavoury creatures, he said, who could see no farther than the ends of their own little noses.

Auntie Minnie was exceedingly short-sighted. And she did have a very small nose. Was it possible that she was a Mercurial? Was Perry a Mercurial too? Was that why he had wanted to be Robbie's friend so much, to prove that the Mercurials were as good as the Moonbabies? Martha had the jigsaw puzzle feeling all over again, even more strongly than before. She felt as if the scattered pieces of the puzzle were beginning to fit themselves together. And she really didn't like the picture they were making.

A Mercurial deputation has been sent to Earth. Uncle Bixbite's voice seemed to echo in her head. The *Mercurials may be closer than you think.* Martha pressed her clammy hands to her cheeks. The Mercurials might already be closer than any of them had even imagined.

The longer she stared at Auntie Minnie, who in turn was staring so venomously at Opal, the more convinced Martha became. And when the pointed top of her headwrap started to tilt and point right at Opal, she was surer than ever. The end of the orange scarf flicked very quickly backwards and then forwards again. It reminded Martha of a scorpion's tail, poised and ready to strike. Something was in there, something alive. Something dangerous.

Opal didn't notice any of this. As far as Martha could tell, she hadn't even seen Auntie Minnie. Garnet had noticed though. All the time Auntie Minnie was there he lay completely flat with his head on his paws, gazing at her with round eyes and licking his lips nervously.

'It's all right, Garnie,' Martha whispered as Perry's aunt finally left the stage. 'She's gone now.' Garnet stopped licking his lips and nuzzled into Martha's legs instead. The poor mingle was quaking with fear. Martha was afraid too, there were goose pimples spreading up her arm, but she said firmly, 'I won't let them hurt you,

Garnie. I won't let them hurt Opal either. I won't!'

Martha was determined to find out exactly what was going on. But the possibility that Minnie and Perry might actually be a pair of the devious demons Uncle Bixbite had described, the very thought of having to fight them filled her with terrible dread. She had no idea how to battle a Mercurial. But Opal would know. She needed to get Opal on her own as soon as possible. She would tell her of her fears and they would work everything out together.

Chapter Eighteen

As soon as the bell rang at the end of the afternoon, Martha began slipping out of her costume. She was desperate to get away but unfortunately Mrs Underedge chose that moment to come and inspect the harp outfit and she had to wait as everyone else filed out of the hall before her.

When she did finally manage to escape, Opal was already bounding off to hockey club with a group of her many friends.

Mum was working so Martha took her books over to A Cut Above and sat at the reception desk by the big salon window. She did her homework in a rush, glancing up all the while to see if Opal was on her way home yet. She needed to speak to her urgently.

Raindrops trickled down the windowpane, chasing one another over the glass. It grew steadily darker outside and there was still no sign of Opal. Martha flicked again and again through the pages of her *Animals of the World* encyclopaedia, looking for something that she guessed wasn't even in there. She had begun to suspect that the animal she was searching for didn't come from her world at all.

Alesha was cutting hair while Mum was calling all the wholesale hair-product suppliers, searching for Luxury Locks hair conditioner. It was the only conditioner that Alesha approved of. She said A Cut Above wouldn't be a cut above anything without it. 'It's a crisis, Mariella,' she said, fanning a clump of her client's hair out across her hand and snipping expertly through it. 'If we don't find some Luxury Locks soon, there's going to be a conditioner catastrophioso! '

'We'll find it,' said Mum, crossing another name off the list in the phone book. 'There must be loads of Luxury Locks out there somewhere. Unless someone's been drinking it all.' She winked at Martha, who smiled and went back to turning the pages of her encyclopaedia.

At last Martha saw Opal hopscotching her way along the pavement with Garnet on her head. Martha jumped up. 'Back in a bit, Mum,' she called. She grabbed her encyclopaedia and raced outside.

'Hello, Best and Only,' said Opal when Martha caught up with her by the Domestipod. 'I was just singing your harp song. It's lovely, isn't it? I can't get it out of my zooming head for some reason. Not that I want to.' She began to sing. Her singing was very loud and very flat.

'No need to be sad, Sir,
No need for you to frown.
No need to be—'

'Opal, stop, please,' said Martha.

'I know, I know,' said Opal. 'I can't do it nearly as well as you. Singing's not a Carnelian strong point if you must know.'

'No,' said Martha. 'It's not that. Opal, I need to talk to you.'

'Oh,' said Opal. 'I see.' She promptly sat down on her doorstep, or the place where her doorstep would have been if she'd had one, and stretched out her legs. 'Fire off, Martha,' she said. 'What's on your brain?'

'Can't you see what's on it?' said Martha. 'You can still read minds, can't you?' Opal had a habit of reading your mind when you least wanted her to and then not reading it all when you needed her to.

'Of course I can still read minds,' said Opal quickly. She leaned forward and peered at Martha closely. 'You're thinking about the Mercurials.' She sat back and flicked away a damp leaf that had settled on her trousers. 'That's a waste of perfectly good headspace. What, in Carnelia's name, are you thinking about them for?'

'I'm worried that they're here,' Martha said. 'In Archwell. Uncle Bixbite said they'd be coming and, Opal, I think they're here already. I think they're planning to hurt you.'

Opal leaned against her green front door. 'What gives you that wondrous notion?' she asked.

Now that Opal was finally listening to her, Martha found it difficult to know where to start. 'Perry,' she began. 'You know, the boy that started school at the same time you did.'

'The one in the cow suit with Robbie?' said Opal. 'That little pip-squirt?'

'Yes,' said Martha.

'What about him?'

Then it all came spilling out. 'There's something funny about him. He's not like other boys. Robbie hated him

151

at first and now he likes him and I can't understand why. I think he might have put Robbie under some sort of spell. And he's got this horrible pet called a locust-grub and I can't find a single one of those in here.' She waved her animal encyclopaedia. 'I'm worried it might be his mingle. Mercurials have mingles too, don't they? Like the Moonbabies? You said all Carnelians had to have them.'

Before Opal could answer, Martha went on. 'And there's his aunt. She's strange too, and she always wears that weird thing on her head and she tried to give me a choker, and she was ever so cross when I said I didn't want it and Garnet was so afraid of her he started trembling and she glared at you in this really horrible way and I . . . I don't like the look in her eyes.' As she finished speaking Garnet flew off Opal's head and landed in Martha's arms. He pushed his nose into the collar of her shirt and kept it there.

Martha took a deep breath. It felt good to have shared her fears at last. Now the two of them could work out what to do next.

To her dismay, Opal laughed.

'Martha,' she guffawed, 'I never knew you were such a worry-worm!'

'What?' said Martha, confused. 'You mean, you don't think they are Mercurials?' She had gabbled everything out so quickly. Maybe she hadn't explained it properly.

Opal stood and folded her arms. 'You've obviously been letting your imagination run rings round you. I've told you before. If there was a Mercurial in Archwell, I'd know about it. They'd stand out like a sore plum. I'm quite sure there's not a single Mercurial in the neighbour-hat.'

'But what if there was?' Martha tried again. 'What if they were tricking you in some way? What if you couldn't recognise them? Uncle Bixbite said they were devious. They might be here, Opal. They might be planning to cover you from head to toe in their hair any day now. I don't want you to be sent to Drabbar!'

Opal raised her cape with her arms so that she looked like a huge bat. 'That,' she said firmly, 'is never going to happen. Stop worrying, Martha. I am the only Carnelian in Archwell. It's a super definite certainty.'

Opal was so confident, it made Martha doubt her own instincts. Perhaps she was jumping to conclusions. She didn't have any real proof that Perry and his aunt were Mercurials. 'Maybe you're right,' she said. 'But there are still things you haven't explained.' She tapped the encyclopaedia. 'That locust-grub for instance. It could be a Mercurial mingle. What if it is? You could be in danger.'

'I don't think so, Best and Only.' Opal strutted up and down. 'I'm absolutely tickety boop and everything's going super-swimmily, don't you think? Garnet's allowed in school. Everybody likes me. Even Mrs U is on my side. And now I've got the title role in the school play. I'm the beanstalk itself. How evil is that!'

'You mean wicked,' said Martha miserably. 'It's wicked, not evil.'

'Right you are,' said Opal. 'How wicked is that!' She batted her eyelashes and the puddles around them fizzed and sparkled with violet stars.

'That's another thing,' said Martha. 'Should you be doing all that?'

'All what?'

'All that stuff with your eyes. Stars and hearts and coloured lights. Doesn't it drain your power? If the Mercurials *do* come and your eyes aren't—'

'You sound like Uncle Bixie,' Opal interrupted. 'He's forever telling me what to do and what not to do and giving me lectures. He's always in my case.'

'Is he?' said Martha quietly, feeling hurt.

'Oh, yes! You're beginning to sound just like him.'

'Am I?'

'You are. The similarity is striking. Uncanny. You're not a Moonbaby aunt in disguise by any chance, are you, Martha?'

'No, of course not!' Opal could be so frustrating sometimes.

'Wouldn't it be funny, though, if you were?' mused Opal. 'Wouldn't it be funny if we turned out to be related? We could be cousins-in-law. Or, I know, better still, we could be star sisters!'

Martha didn't like being compared to Uncle Bixbite, it made her feel as if Opal thought she was trying to boss her around, but she did like the idea of being Opal's star sister. It made her feel much better. 'Do you want to meet up tomorrow,' she said on the spur of the moment. 'After school? After you've done your club?'

'I'd love to,' said Opal. They smiled at one another and for one delicious moment Martha felt herself beginning to glow, as if a forgotten ember inside her was being rekindled.

Then Opal pulled a roll of paper from her inside pocket and spoiled the moment. 'Trouble is, I've got all these other people waiting to do things with me. Look, I've a list here as long as your leg.' She unrolled the paper which was covered in her scrawly handwriting. She was right, the list was as long as Martha's leg, longer even. Opal examined it, sucking her finger. 'I can probably fit you in in December,' she said. 'Or maybe after that, in the Fresh Year.'

Martha bit her lip.

'Why are you eating your mouth like that?' said Opal. 'It's not that human jealousy pudding feeling again, is it?'

Martha did feel jealous. She'd worked so hard to look after Opal, to be her Best and Only Friend, and now she was being left out. She felt as if she didn't matter to Opal at all. Opal's words were like slaps. They made her feel sore and they made her angry. Big surges of anger rolled up inside her. She felt like ripping that list out of Opal's hand and tearing it into tiny shreds. Why didn't Opal see? Why didn't she even take the trouble to look?

'No,' she said, through gritted teeth. 'I'm not jealous.'

'That's all right then,' said Opal. She plucked Garnet from Martha's arms. 'Well, I'd better be getting in. It's school tomorrow and I need to catch up on my brainy sleep.' The door to the Domestipod slid open. 'See you tomorrow then, Best and—'

Martha cut her off. 'No!' she shouted. 'Stop calling me that, Opal! Stop calling me "Best and Only". It isn't even true. It doesn't mean anything. I'm not your *best* friend at all, am I?' She flicked the unrolled paper still flapping in Opal's hand. 'And I'm obviously not your *only* one! I'm not your best and only anything!'

Opal's eyes widened in surprise. 'Martha,' she began. 'You'll always—'

Martha cut her off. 'You said you wanted my advice,

155

but you don't. You never take it. You never spend time with me. It's pretty clear you don't even want to be with me. Well, fine! I hope you enjoy being on Earth. I hope you have a great time but you can do it on your own. You can look out for yourself from now on, Opal Moonbaby, because I'm not going to. Goodbye!'

She didn't give Opal a chance to reply. She didn't want her to see the tears that were already springing from her eyes. She turned and ran through the darkness all the way back to the salon, clutching her encyclopaedia to her chest.

Chapter Eighteen

The weather turned bitterly cold the next week, as autumn suddenly became winter. Each morning Martha wrapped herself in her thick winter coat and her long woolly scarf. She wore her hat pulled low over her ears and she kept her head down as she walked, but the wind still whipped at her cheeks and tore at her clothing. By the time she reached school her toes were painful and her fingers were red and raw. It was the worst kind of cold. The kind when the world looks hard and grey. The leaves were all gone and the trees were bare. There wasn't even any snow or frost to decorate the walls and hedges along the way to school.

They were rehearsing for *Jack and the Beanstalk* every single day. Most people were excited but Martha wasn't. She wasn't enjoying the rehearsals at all; to her each one seemed to go on longer than the last. As the performance approached Mrs Underedge grew crosser and crosser. She was particularly cross with Martha because she never started singing when she was supposed to. Martha found it difficult to concentrate on the play because she was concentrating so hard on not thinking about

Opal. If she did think about her, Martha's thoughts soon strayed onto what had happened between them that night outside the Domestipod. When she thought about that she couldn't trust herself not to cry so she tried not to dwell on it.

Martha probably wouldn't have remembered to sing at all if it wasn't for Jessie giving her a nudge and hissing, 'You're on!'

There were just two days to go now before the performance. According to Robbie, Perry's Auntie Minnie had finished the weaving she was doing for the backdrop. She was going to bring it in for the dress rehearsal the following morning. Robbie had had a sneak preview of the weaving but he wouldn't say what it looked like. He and Perry kept tapping the sides of their noses and telling everyone they would have to wait and see because it was a surprisey-wisey. Robbie was spending all his time with Perry now. Martha had tried telling him of her suspicions that Perry and his aunt were Mercurials but he had laughed and said she was off her head. When Robbie was with Perry, Martha tried to ignore both of them as much as possible.

She tried to ignore Opal too. She had avoided her quite successfully so far. It wasn't hard. Opal seemed keen to talk to her and often called her name, but there were so many people vying for Opal's attention that it was easy for Martha to sidestep her and slip away. And if Opal tried to catch her eye during rehearsals Martha was careful never to meet her gaze.

She couldn't ignore Garnet though. Whenever he sat next to her on the giant's table he would whimper and say *chi-wi-chi* as if he was trying to get her to do something, or to show her that he was afraid. She tried to comfort him by patting him and fondling his ears, his real ears, not his paper rabbit ones, though it never seemed to do the trick. Stroking Garnet was usually comforting to Martha too, but these days it didn't seem to make either of them feel much better.

'What's the matter, Martha?' Mum asked that evening. Martha was sitting too close to the telly, hugging her legs and glowering. She wasn't focusing on what was on.

'Nothing,' she said, resting her chin on her knees.

Mum was in the middle of making cupcakes. They were for the night of the performance, for the audience to eat in the interval. Mum hadn't been able to help with the rehearsals for *Jack and the Beanstalk* so she had offered to bake instead. She came and sat on the arm of the sofa, a tea towel slung over her arm. 'Doesn't look like nothing to me,' she said. 'You've been going round with a long face for days now. What's it all about? Have you fallen out with your new friend? Is that it?'

'No,' Martha lied. If she admitted that she had fallen out with Opal, then Mum would want to know the details. If she wasn't careful she might let the whole story spill out. She was angry with Opal but she was still determined not to give away her secret. 'Opal and I are fine.'

Mum went on. 'She's quite a character, isn't she, that Opal? I expect she's very popular at school.'

'Mmm,' said Martha. She swallowed an annoying lump that kept coming up into her throat and stared harder at the television.

'I think I'd be feeling a bit envious if I were you. After all, you made friends with her first, didn't you? It must be difficult having to share her with everyone else.'

Martha didn't reply but Mum kept talking as if she

hadn't noticed.

'It's a shame things aren't working out for you with Opal. It's been so great for Robbie, having Perry around.' Mum picked a bit of cake mix off the tea towel. 'Robbie's round there right now. He's even persuaded me to let him go for a sleepover tomorrow. Not the best timing since it's your performance the next night but there we are. I've made him promise he'll get plenty of sleep.'

The pips went on the oven timer and Mum stood up. 'Perry's an odd little chap though, I must say. I'd never have guessed he was going to be Robbie's type.'

'Perry's horrible!' Martha burst out angrily. 'He's a mega-creep!'

'Oh, now,' scolded Mum. 'I know you're feeling a bit jealous, Martha, but there's no need to be mean.'

Martha picked up the remote and shot it at the telly, switching it off. 'Why does everyone think I'm jealous all the time? I'm not jealous at all.'

Mum didn't say anything, she went back to her baking, but Martha could tell from her face that she didn't believe her. 'I'm not! I'm not JEALOUS!' She stormed off to the bedroom followed only by the insistent beeping of the oven timer.

Martha threw herself down on her bunk. 'I'm not jealous!' she said again, although she knew she was really. She was jealous of Opal's other friends, jealous of Robbie and Perry, jealous of everybody. Angrily, she rammed her fists into her pockets. There was something in one of them, right down in the corner of the lining. A squashed-up piece of paper, hardened into a ball.

It's like my heart, thought Martha. That's gone all tight and hard too. She pressed the compacted paper between her palms. If you could touch a jealous heart this was what it would feel like.

She fingered the ball, flicking at a tab of the paper that had come free. Whatever it was had been through the washing machine, maybe more than once. She picked at the paper and unfurled it, spreading it out on her knee. It was scrunched and faded. The illuminated initial on the front was very faint, but it was still recognisable. It was the list of Tips and Pointers she had written for Opal when she had first arrived at school. That all seemed a very long time ago now.

As far as Martha knew, Opal hadn't even read the list and she had broken every single one of the rules almost straightaway. She hadn't taken any of Martha's advice and what had happened? Nothing. Nothing at all. 'Opal Moonbaby doesn't need me,' Martha said aloud. 'She's fine without me. She always has been and she always will be.'

All the same, she couldn't help reading the tips through one more time. Smoothing the list out, Martha caught sight of her own name at the bottom. She saw what she had written there.

Tips by Martha Stephens. Your Best and Only Friend.

Martha screwed the list up again and lobbed it into the waste bin. That was the best place for it now. She got into bed. It wasn't bedtime. She hadn't brushed her teeth. She was still fully dressed, Robbie wasn't even home yet, but Martha didn't care. She pulled the duvet up over her head. She didn't want to be awake any more.

Under the covers, Martha screwed her eyes shut. 'Not best,' she whispered. 'And not only. Best and only NOTHING!'

Chapter Nineteen

'**O**pal!'

Martha cried out as she woke, gasping for breath. It was already morning.

She had been dreaming about Opal. It was a terrifying dream. Opal was caught in a huge black and orange cobweb. She was being bound up in it and the harder she tried to free herself, the tighter the web grew and the more tangled she became. As the web clung to Opal's face, her eyes began to fade. Their shining violet irises turned drab, grey and unseeing. Just as the light was seeping out of them for good, Martha had woken.

She tried to sit up but she was trapped in her duvet, her arms clamped firmly to her sides. She was rolled so tightly she might have been a sausage wrapped in pastry, ready for the oven. Wriggling, she managed to free one of her arms and pull the duvet out from under her. She pushed it off and felt the cool air running over her body and her now rumpled school uniform. It was a relief to be free but she was still left with a horrible sweaty sick feeling.

Her first thought was to go and find out if Opal was all right. The dream seemed so real, she was scared that

something terrible really had happened to her. Then she reminded herself of the worries she had had before, of her suspicions about Perry and Auntie Minnie. Opal had laughed when she had told her about them. Martha didn't like Perry and his aunt, she didn't trust them an inch, but they hadn't actually *done* anything. So maybe they weren't Mercurials after all. Opal said they weren't and Opal ought to know. In any case, it was nothing to do with Martha. Opal had told her very clearly that she could look after herself. Martha had made a promise to Uncle Bixbite but if Opal wouldn't listen to her, what could she do about it? Especially, she reminded herself, since they had stopped being friends now.

'It's none of my business,' she said aloud.

The mattress jolted beneath her.

'Are you nutty? I'm asking Mum to get me my own room.'

Robbie was in the bunk below, balancing on his shoulders and kicking at Martha's mattress. She leaned over to look at him. 'You were talking in your sleep,' he complained. 'You were raving about Opal and spiders or something. I think your brain's disintegrating.'

He let his legs down and lay on his back, fiddling with the bracelet that Perry had given him. 'At least I'll get a bit of peace tonight.'

He got out of bed and started rummaging around in his belongings, collecting up Yoyo, an assortment of playing cards and his secret stash of sweets. He whistled happily as he crammed the things into a backpack along with his sleeping bag.

'Auntie Minnie's bringing in the weaving later,' he said. 'There's hardly any lessons because it's the dress rehearsal all afternoon, and then I get to go to Perry's for the whole night. This is going to be one of the most immense days ever!'

Martha groaned and rubbed her stomach.

She couldn't eat her breakfast. She sat with her elbow on the table, cradling her head in her hand; it felt too heavy to stay up by itself. She watched Robbie making short work of his cereal and four slices of toast and strawberry jam.

Mum put her hand on Martha's forehead. 'You're not hot,' she said, 'but you don't look too clever. What are your symptoms?'

'I can't go to school,' replied Martha. 'I can't.'

'You'll miss the dress rehearsal,' said Robbie.

'So what? I know my song and I've worn my costume loads already. I don't need any more rehearsing.'

'Better to miss the dress rehearsal than the performance,' said Mum, reaching for the phone. 'I think you could do with a rest. I'll tell school I'm keeping you off and I bet you'll be right as rain tomorrow.'

Mum said Martha ought to be in bed really but she couldn't miss work to look after her so Martha had to go to the salon too. Alesha wasn't too pleased to see Martha arrive wearing her dressing gown. She had flung it on over yesterday's school uniform because she felt too groggy to get dressed properly. Alesha made her stay in the storeroom, out of sight.

Alesha was even more grumpy than usual. Martha could hear her, bossing Mum around and moaning about the shortage of Luxury Locks.

'My clients need that stuff, Mariella,' she whined. 'Egg yolks and aloes are the best treatment for hair that's tired and fatiguo. There's nothing else like it.' Martha could hear Mum too, speaking in a quiet calming tone. It didn't do any good. Alesha was having a bad day and she didn't care who knew it.

'I've got such a splitting headache,' she said, clomping into the storeroom at lunchtime. 'Even the tiniest noise sounds like an avalancho in my head. I think I'm getting a migraine.'

'Not like you to get headaches,' said Mum, following her in and taking a rose-hip teabag from the box on the counter.'

Alesha winced. 'Oh, stop rustling those teabags so violentissimo, Mariella! You're making it worse!'

'Sorry,' said Mum, making a face at Martha.

'I think it must be the dream I had last night,' Alesha went on. 'I woke up feeling so 'orriblo. I still do. It was a crazymondo dream too. About that girl, the one that lives in the purple cabin.'

'Opal?' said Martha. 'You dreamed about Opal Moonbaby?'

'Yes I did. Don't ask me why, I hardly know the girl. Poor thing, though. It was terrible. She was being suffocated or something.'

'Suffocated?' Martha sat stock-still, staring at Alesha, waiting for her to say more.

'Yes, it was well weirdissimo.' Alesha rubbed her forehead. 'She was being smothered by some kind of netting or webbing.'

'Like a cobweb,' said Martha quietly.

'Right,' said Alesha. 'Just like a cobweb. Only it wasn't cobweb-coloured. It was orange and black. Ooh, it was horrible, all over her face and everywhere. And then her eyes went from being bright and shiny to sort of blanko and dead. That's when I woke up.' Alesha shuddered. 'I haven't been right since.'

Martha felt as if a hundred baby spiders were walking up and down the back of her neck.

A double dream.

Never ignore double dreams. There's always wit and wisdom in them.

Shakily, she got to her feet. This changed everything. She knew now, without the smallest doubt, that she had been right all along. It was Opal who had been wrong. Opal should have listened. Martha should have made her listen.

'I need to go to school,' she said. 'I need to go there now.'

Mum put down her cup of tea. 'But you're not well. Why?'

Martha couldn't say it was because she and Alesha had had a double dream. She couldn't say that double dreams were omens of the future. She couldn't say that she had ignored one double dream already and that she wasn't going to make the same mistake again.

'Opal needs me,' she said under her breath.

'What's that?' said Mum.

'I mean, I need to be at the dress rehearsal,' she said. 'I've just remembered. Mrs Underedge said the whole cast has to be there today. I need to go.'

She ran straight out of the storeroom and flung open the salon door.

'Martha!' Mum called. 'Wait! What about your coat? You haven't had any lunch.'

'Not hungry,' she called back over her shoulder. Icy

air hit her face as she charged out of the salon but she hardly noticed. She ran down the road towards the pedestrian crossing, her dressing gown flying out behind her.

The first double dream Martha had ever had in her life left her with a feeling of hope, a feeling that something good was about to happen. She had ignored it and Opal and the Domestipod had appeared soon afterwards. This second dream was having a very different effect. It made her feel as if something dreadful was on its way. Something to do with Opal.

Whatever Opal thought, whatever Opal said, whether they were friends or whether they weren't, Opal was in terrible danger and she needed help.

Martha ran through the school gates and across the deserted playground. Lunch must already be over. She sprinted on, past Miss Brocklebank's office, down the long corridor to the school hall, going as fast as she could. She prayed that she wouldn't be too late.

Chapter Twenty

Martha barged open the doors of the school hall and came to an abrupt halt. As the doors swung to and fro behind her, she doubled over, hands on her knees, trying to catch her breath.

The hall was empty. Apart from one thing.

A cobweb.

Black and orange and gigantic, just like the one in her dream. It hung at the back of the platform, stretched right across the wall, dominating the stage, dominating the whole hall. It was nothing like the rest of the scenery, which was mostly made out of painted cardboard boxes. It didn't look as if it had anything to do with the story of Jack and the Beanstalk. It looked as if it belonged to the scariest, most poisonous spider in the whole world.

Martha found herself walking towards the cobweb. She felt compelled to go near it as if she was a tiny pin and the cobweb was a powerful magnet drawing her in. Before she knew it she had climbed up onto the stage and was touching it.

The web towered over her. It was so tall, she couldn't even reach its centre, which was densely woven and

matted, with no gaps for air to float through. The web felt wiry and strong, like coarse wool or very thin rope. Some of the threads were straight and shiny and stitched in tightly. Others coiled outwards like springs. Martha pulled one; it stretched taut in her fingers and then slipped away from her, bouncing firmly back into place. The thread felt strangely powerful, almost as if it had a will of its own. Martha tried to imagine what it would feel like if the web was covering her face, its thick rough mesh pressing down on her mouth and nose. She trembled. She wasn't out of breath any longer but her heart was beating faster than when she had first come into the hall. She stepped slowly backwards and clambered down from the stage, all the time keeping her eyes fixed on the cobweb. It didn't feel safe to turn away from it. She kept walking backwards through the hall until she stumbled over something.

She sat heavily on the floor, her legs hooked awkwardly over the obstacle that had tripped her. It was a large shopping bag. The handles had fallen to the sides, and the bag was gaping open. Martha saw immediately that it was jammed full of bottles. Identical plastic bottles. A dozen of them. Maybe more. She lifted one up and looked at the label.

Luxury Locks: with egg yolk and aloes. For maximum volume and strength.

It was hair conditioner. Loads and loads of hair conditioner. The same type that Alesha and Mum used at the salon, the type they were having so much trouble getting hold of.

At once, Martha let go of the bottle, as if it had burned her. No one needed that much hair conditioner. No one on Earth. No human would buy up all the conditioner in Archwell. But someone whose power was in their hair might do that.

A Mercurial might.

'Hello, my little honey pot.'

Martha jumped. She looked up to see Perry's Auntie Minnie staring down at her.

'Feeling better, are we?' A tendril of dark orange hair protruded from her headwrap. It dropped down over one side of her glasses, and bounced there, like a spring. Auntie Minnie twitched her cheek and the hair sprang back into the headwrap. It seemed to do it all by itself but Auntie Minnie reached up and tucked the last little bit of hair away with her fingers.

Martha looked up at the cobweb again. She knew now what it was made of.

Mercurial hair.

Enough Mercurial hair to cover a Moonbaby from head to toe.

Auntie Minnie saw her looking at the cobweb and said, 'What do you think of my weaving? I put a great deal of myself into that cobweb, you know.'

'Yes,' Martha managed to say. 'I do know.' She stared at Auntie Minnie, feeling as if all the blood was draining from her face.

'By the way, sweetie-pattie,' Auntie Minnie went on, taking something from her pocket. 'Have you changed your mind about my little gifty yet?'

Martha looked at the choker dangling from Auntie Minnie's hand. She realised that must be made of Mercurial hair too. And if the choker was made of hair, so was Robbie's friendship bracelet, the one Perry had given him. She shook her head. 'No,' she whispered. 'I haven't.'

Anger darted into Auntie Minnie's black eyes and Martha was relieved to hear the chatter of voices coming along the corridor.

Robbie and Perry came in first. They had the cow suit draped around their shoulders and Perry was leading Robbie along by his friendship bracelet, which he held pinched between two pudgy fingers.

'Hi, Martha,' said Robbie. 'You made it then. What do you think of the weaving?'

Martha couldn't answer but Perry said, in a peculiar breathy voice, 'It's perfect-werfect!'

'Yeah,' said Robbie. 'Mind you, I wouldn't fancy meeting the spider that made it!'

Perry smirked. He and his aunt exchanged glittering glances that sent shivers scurrying up and down Martha's spine.

The rest of the cast poured through the double doors, all in full costume, ready to complete the dress rehearsal.

'Ah, Martha,' said Mrs Underedge. 'Good of you to join us. Although you might have remembered to remove your . . . *night attire*.' Martha had forgotten she was still in her dressing gown. Quickly she took it off. She rolled it up and stood clutching it self-consciously as she scanned the cast for Opal. There was no sign of her.

Mrs Underedge clapped her hands. 'Places, everyone,' she said.

Martha was just wondering if she could sidle away and look for Opal when Jessie came over with the harp costume. 'Are you OK, Martha?' she said. 'Here,

I'll help you put this on. We're having photos done.' She had hardly lifted the straps onto Martha's shoulders before they were both swept forward as everyone else surged onto the stage, eager to be in the production photographs. Martha took her place on the giant's table, still looking everywhere for Opal.

'She's gone to borrow the camera from Mr Morris,' said Jessie. Martha looked at her in surprise. It was as if Jessie was reading her thoughts, but of course Opal was the only one who could really do that.

Opal came in at last, carrying Garnet and the school camera.

'Here's the snapper, Mrs U,' she said.

'Thank you, Opal,' said Mrs Underedge, taking the camera from her. Opal made her way towards the stage. She didn't seem to be moving as quickly as normal and her hair was wilting a little, perhaps weighed down by the orange runner-bean flower she had pinned to it. Then she caught sight of Martha and her eyes lit up.

'Hello, Best and . . .' She stopped herself. 'Hello, Martha,' she said.

Garnet jumped straight out of her arms and raced towards the giant's table. He was so keen to get there that Martha saw his wings begin to unfurl as if he was about to take off and fly to her. He leaped into her lap and nuzzled her tummy. She stroked his fur but she kept her eyes on Opal and held her gaze. This was no time for looking away. Martha didn't speak out loud. She spoke with her thoughts because what she had to say now was for Opal's ears only.

Opal, she thought. *Listen to me.*

Opal blinked her violet eyes questioningly. She

seemed somehow to grasp the deadly seriousness of what Martha was trying to say to her, and she waited.

Fixing Opal's eyes with her own, Martha let all her thoughts and fears and realisations come flooding into her head, like a slide show, for Opal to watch.

She thought of Uncle Bixbite's warning to Opal that the Mercurials might be coming to Archwell in search of her. She thought of Perry and the day he had arrived in school, so soon after Opal's own arrival. She thought of his strange behaviour in the school playground when he had asked her to pick up two of his hairs. She thought of Beryl, the horrible creature he kept with him at all times. She thought of Auntie Minnie and the mysterious movements she had seen inside her headwrap. She thought of the horrible, hungry stares that Auntie Minnie had sent in Opal's direction. She thought of all the conditioner lined up in the shopping bag. She thought of the choker that Auntie Minnie kept trying to give her, and the bracelet that was fastened to Robbie's wrist. She thought of the awful double dream and the way Opal had suffocated in it. She relived for Opal the feeling of horror that had filled her when she first saw the terrible cobweb that Auntie Minnie had woven.

Finally she switched her thoughts over and thought of Opal herself. She thought how it didn't matter what Opal said to her, or even whether they were destined to be best friends. She thought instead of how Opal was in trouble and if there was one thing Martha needed to do, it was to help, to keep her safe. That was what Martha wanted. She wanted to stop the Mercurials from covering her from head to toe in their hair until she lost all her powers. She wanted to stop her being sentenced to a lonely life on Drabbar. She had promised Uncle Bixbite that she would do that. And she would, whatever else happened.

You don't have to be best friends with me if you don't want to, Opal. You can be friends with whoever you like. But right now you're in terrible danger, and you have to let me help you.

Martha let out her breath. She realised she had been holding it all the time as she relayed her thoughts to Opal. Garnet, still on her lap, let out a small *cheee* of his own, as if to say, 'That's exactly what I've been trying to tell you too.'

Opal did something then that Martha had never seen her do before.

She blushed. Deeply, pinkly, just like a human. She put her hands up to her cheeks, clearly shocked to be experiencing such a strange sensation. She looked as if she would like to say something, but Martha couldn't read minds, and anyway, Mrs Underedge was shouting. She was shouting at Opal; she hadn't done that for ages.

'Opal! Opal Moonbaby!' she screeched. 'For the *umpteenth* time! Will you turn round? We are trying to take some production photographs and we don't want to see the back of the beanstalk. Turn round at once and show us your green shoots!'

Opal turned and Mrs Underedge raised the camera. Martha was worried the flash would set Opal's eyes off and that there would be a dazzling light show. Camera flashes had always made Opal's eyes go crazy in the past. That was all they needed now.

But nothing happened. Mrs Underedge took several photos and nothing happened at all. Martha thought

Opal must have kept her eyes closed for the whole time. Mrs Underedge was so agitated about the impending performance that she didn't even notice.

☆ ☆ ☆

'Don't go to Perry's tonight. Please, Robbie. You mustn't!'

Martha grabbed Robbie's arm. Mrs Underedge had kept them so busy practising the curtain call, she hadn't had a chance to speak to him during the rehearsal, and she was only just in time to catch him before he left school. He was collecting his overnight bag from his peg, while Perry waited for him on the school climbing frame.

Robbie frowned. 'Are you kidding? Auntie Minnie says I can sleep in the driver's cab tonight if I want. There's no way I'm going to miss that.'

Waves of dread washed over Martha. 'You mustn't go. Robbie, it's dangerous!'

'Course it's not. The motorhome doesn't actually go anywhere. It's completely still.'

'Robbie, don't go and stay with them. Please. I'm begging you!'

'Why not?'

'Because . . . because they're Mercurials. Perry and his Auntie Minnie. They're not what they seem. They're only pretending. They're—'

'Not this again!' Robbie laughed in her face. 'Don't be stupid, Martha,' he said, fingering the bracelet Perry had given him. 'Perry's really nice. So's Auntie Minnie. I mean if they were Mercurials, I wouldn't like them, would I? I'm not a total idiot.'

He was about to run off when he stopped and took a chocolate raisin box out of his pocket. 'I nearly forgot,' he said. 'Can you look after Mark and Kevin and Clive for me? There's some blood in an egg cup by my bed. Can you give them that?' He pressed the box into Martha's hand. 'And keep them out of Mum's way,' he called as he ran off to join Perry, who was hanging upside down on the climbing frame, swinging from side to side like a clock's pendulum. Martha stayed by the pegs and watched helplessly as the two of them ran through the school gate without a backward glance. Other people poured past her on the way out of school, bumping her with bags and shoulders as they went.

Then a hand brushed hers. Long fingers laced themselves between Martha's fingers, and a warm palm pressed into her cold one. Martha breathed in and a deliciously familiar smell of sparklers and hot pepper filled her nostrils.

Martha felt a tear come to her eye. To stop it falling, she concentrated on the hand that was curled round hers. She let her fingers bend and squeezed the hand back.

Chapter Twenty-one

Martha and Opal went straight to A Cut Above. Martha could see from Mum's face that she would have been in for a massive telling off if it wasn't for the fact that she had Opal with her.

'Fancy running to school in your dressing gown like that!' was all Mum said.

'It's a very warm dressing gown,' said Martha. 'It's as good as my coat, really.'

Mum tutted. 'How are you feeling now, anyway?'

'Oh, loads better, thanks. Can I go to Opal's for a sleepover? Robbie's having a sleepover. Can I have one too?'

'No you can't!' said Mum. 'You've been feeling poorly and you've got *Jack and the Beanstalk* tomorrow night.'

'Oh, please let Martha come, Marie Stephens,' said Opal, putting her arm through Martha's. 'It would be so magnificently splendidly awesome.'

Mum looked doubtful. 'Well, I'm glad to see you two have made it up at last.' she said. Then she sighed. 'Your uncle's at home, is he, Opal?'

'Oh yes,' said Opal. 'He's at home all right.' It wasn't

a lie. Uncle Bixbite was at home. At home on Carnelia.

'OK, then,' said Mum. 'I suppose so.' Martha and Opal were halfway to the Domestipod before she added, 'But make sure you get some sleep!'

✫ ✫ ✫

Opal's green front door slid open at once, as if the Domestipod had been waiting for them.

Once they were inside, Garnet unfurled his wings and fluttered onto Martha's shoulder. He began purring and kneading at her jacket. Then he looked sharply at Opal and swivelled his head right round on his neck. *'Chigga-chee-chee!'*

'All right, Garnie,' said Opal. 'I know. I've been a complete and utter nincompooper, and I owe Martha a heart-meant apology.'

'Chichee,' said Garnet with a little snarl.

'Keep your fur on!' said Opal to the indignant mingle. 'I'm doing it, aren't I?'

But Garnet flew round and round, diving at Opal's head until she was forced to kneel on the floor. He seemed satisfied then and went and perched on the light shade. The pink of the Domestipod walls deepened a shade or two, and sad-sounding violin music began to play.

'Martha Stephens,' said Opal, looking up at her with large, sorrowful and very sincere eyes. 'I have been a big gooseberry fool.'

'Have you?' said Martha.

'I'll say I have. I've been having lots of fun settling in on Earth, going to school, making friends. I love making friends. But I realise now that I've made about fifty-five too many. I've been collecting new friends the way human beings collect teapots or stamps. And I've been forgetting the one person who really cares about me. My one true friend. You've been looking out for me all this time, Martha, and I've been completely neglecting you. And now I feel . . . I feel . . .' Opal sprang to her feet. 'It's happening again,' she said, patting wildly at her cheeks, which were now as pink as the walls of her little house. 'I must be ill. My face has gone hot. I must have an Earth fever. I might need a doctor or a hospital or, or . . . a thermometer!' She hopped around so madly, anyone would think she was on fire.

Martha couldn't help smiling. 'You're not ill, Opal,' she said. 'You're embarrassed. You're blushing. Everyone does it when they feel ashamed.'

'A-shamed,' repeated Opal, trying out the word. She blinked her eyes, looking up the meaning in her dictionary. 'Yes, that's it exactly. I feel guilty and embarrassed because I've done a foolish thing. Lots of foolish things actually.'

She smiled sheepishly and took out her Human Handybook. 'I haven't got anything about ashamed or guilty or embarrassed in here yet,' she said, waving the notepad at Martha and taking out her pencil. 'I'd better add them to the list.' She flicked through the pages. 'Oh,' she said. 'I've run out of space.'

'Maybe you need a bigger notebook,' said Martha.

'Maybe,' said Opal. She sounded almost meek, which was unusual for her. 'Martha?' she said, kneeling down again and looking up at her appealingly.

'Yes, Opal?'

'I've been a prize twit-nit and I'm really very, very

sorry.' She blinked her long eyelashes. 'Do you think you can ever forgive me?'

Opal was gazing at her so beseechingly, she reminded Martha of a naughty puppy waiting to find out if it would be punished or patted. It would be difficult not to forgive a puppy. And it was impossible not to forgive Opal Moonbaby.

'I forgive you,' Martha said.

Opal shuffled forward on her knees and hugged Martha's legs.

'I thought you did,' she said. 'But I wanted to hear you say it in person, just to make sure. Do you really, definitely forgive me?'

'Yes,' said Martha. She put her hands on Opal's shoulders and looked into her eyes. 'I really, definitely do.'

'Oh zippedee-do-dogs!' Opal cried, throwing her head back. 'Then I'm the happiest alien alive! Thanks, Best and Only.'

She was about to hug her again but Martha put up a hand. 'There's one condition,' she said. 'I don't want you to call me that any more. I'm still your best friend, Opal. I hope I am anyway. I'm not your only one, though. Can you just call me Martha from now on?'

'Dokey okey,' said Opal, 'Anything you say, Best and .. . I mean, Martha.' She gave Martha one last squeeze and Martha squeezed her back. It felt so good being true friends again after all this time. Martha could almost feel her heart softening in her chest. But there were things to be getting on with.

'OK,' she said, gently pushing Opal away. 'Now that's sorted, we've got a job to do. We've got problems, remember? Big problems.'

'You're absolutely right,' said Opal. 'There's no time to be losing.' She glanced at the wall and the laundry box skittered forward across the floor, stopping smartly in front of them. Martha lifted the lid and found the balled-up towel Opal had shoved there at the end of Uncle Bixbite's visit. It was covered in ornate white lettering, none of which Martha could read, since it was all written in Carnelian. She passed the towel to Opal.

'Right,' said Opal. 'These are the Mercurial aunts missing from Carnelia.' She began to recite. 'Apatite, Malachite, Melanite, Morganite, Mineral, Tourmaline and Zircon.' She looked at Martha. 'No Minnies there,' she said. 'Let's try the nephews and nieces. Agate, Obsidian . . .'

'Wait,' said Martha. 'What was that one in the middle? Mineral, wasn't it? Minnie could be short for Mineral.'

'By Georgie, you're right!' exclaimed Opal. 'Mineral Mercurial is here on Earth. So who's that young whippysnappy she's brought with her?' She began to read aloud. 'Agate, Obsidian, Peridot . . .'

'Perry!' shouted Martha. 'Perry could be Peridot.'

'Hmm,' said Opal. 'They certainly fit the descriptions, although we can't see what their hair looks like. It says here that Mineral's hair is of the contorted variety. Orange and black, and very, very curly.'

'Yes!' cried Martha. 'It is. I've seen it. A bit fell out of her headwrap, at the dress rehearsal!'

'And their mingles,' Opal read on, 'are called Onyx and . . .' she scanned the towel with her eyes, 'Beryl.'

'That's it!' said Martha. 'Perry, or Peridot, or whatever his name is, he's got a locust-grub thing called Beryl. I told you about her before. She's revolting. Does it say anything about Onyx?'

'Only that he's mainly snake,' said Opal, 'with a drop of hatchetfish and a dash of scorpion.'

Martha couldn't contain herself. 'I've seen him too,' she said. 'Bits of him anyway. He's hiding in Mineral's headscarf. I'm sure of it. But why didn't you spot them, Opal? Why didn't you Z-ray them with your eyes? If I could see what was going on, why couldn't you? You have been looking after your eyes, haven't you?'

Opal shrugged. ''Course I have. It's not me. It's them. They must have some sort of disguise or an eye-blocking device. Maybe Mineral and Peridot Mercurial are cleverer than I thought because they just look like normal human beings to me.'

'And to Robbie,' said Martha. 'He's with them right now. He's staying the night on their motorhome.' She nibbled anxiously at her fingernails.

'Motorhome, eh?' said Opal, stroking her chin. 'Where is this motorhome, then?'

'Robbie said it was behind the bus depot. Just across the park.'

'Then we'd better get over there, lickety splitety,' said Opal as the clothes rail flew out from the wall. 'We need to find out exactly what we're up across.' She tossed a cape to Martha and threw another over her own shoulders. 'Let's go!' she said, and they ran out of the door together with Garnet flitting behind them.

Chapter Twenty-two

The route to the bus depot was very straightforward. You just had to follow the path that cut across the middle of the park, head out through the gate at the other end, turn left and you were there. It was straightforward in daylight anyway. After dark it was quite another matter. There was no moon visible behind the clouds and Martha couldn't see the path at all.

'Don't worry,' said Opal. 'I'll switch on my light beams.'

Two violet lights, the same oval shape as Opal's eyes, appeared on the ground ahead. The beams weren't very bright though and they couldn't get along very fast, but at least Martha could see where she was putting her feet now.

The gate at the far edge of the park was already locked for the night so they had to feel their way along the railings until they found a gap big enough to squeeze through.

Once they were on the pavement they hurried on, passing the bus depot wall that loomed up, huge as a mountain.

'This is it,' whispered Martha when they came to an opening in the wall. Peering through into a large yard, she could just make out some huge dustbins and a pile

of old crates. In front of them stood the dark mounded shape of the motorhome.

It was parked at a strange angle right across the yard as if it had swerved to a stop, just centimetres from the depot wall. Even in the dim light, Martha recognised it. It was the same vehicle that had almost run Robbie over all those weeks ago, on the day they had first seen the Domestipod. Auntie Minnie, or Mineral, if it was really she who had been at the wheel, was evidently a very bad driver.

There were lights on in the motorhome and a movement from inside made Martha duck, pulling Opal down with her. They were all in there, she realised. Mineral, Peridot, Beryl and Onyx. Martha's legs felt weak as she crouched down. They had made it to the Mercurials' hideout but what were they going to do now? How was Opal going to fight them? She imagined a battle of lasers and light rays as Opal had once described. Opal was going to dazzle-kick the Mercurials all the way back to Carnelia. But would the Mercurials fight back? And what with? Lassos probably, and ropes and trapping nets made of their horrible hair.

They crouched there for what seemed like minutes. Martha's heart beat so loudly in her chest, she was sure the Mercurials would hear it and that they would be discovered, but nothing happened. After a while, she realised that although the motorhome was brightly lit, and she could see inside it easily, the yard itself was extremely dark and she and Opal couldn't be seen at all.

Encouraged by this, Martha signalled to Opal and they crept closer. Martha put her hands on the vehicle's great bonnet. Her fingers met a strange shaggy material.

She parted a few tassels; the surface underneath was bumpy and dry as if it had been baked in clay. Using the wheel as a step, she pulled herself up. At once, she came face to face with Robbie, sitting in the driver's cab in his pyjamas. He was perching on his rolled up sleeping bag, using it as a booster seat. Even so, he could barely reach the steering wheel, which he was turning this way and that, pretending to drive.

'Hurry up, Perry,' he shouted, not seeing Martha or Opal. 'We're nearly at Brighton.'

'With you in a minutey-winutey,' called a muffled voice. Peridot's voice. Coming from behind the door that led to the main compartment of the motorhome.

'OK,' Robbie called back. 'But don't be longy-wongy, will you?' He heaved the wheel sharply to one side. 'Road hog!' he shouted at some imaginary driver on the imaginary road in front of him. As he pulled the wheel back Martha caught sight of the bracelet of hair, sticking out of his pyjama sleeve.

'Why is he talking in that strange way?' Opal whispered. 'All that longy-wongy stuff?'

'I don't know for sure,' said Martha. 'But I think it has something to do with that.' She pointed at the bracelet of woven black and brown strands. I think that's Mercurial hair. And it's working on him like a spell.'

'Yes. He's been brain-swabbed all right,' said Opal. She stroked the dark brown bonnet of the motorhome. 'And the Mercurials are definitely here. This is one of their space-domes. They've coated it in their hair so that I wouldn't see it. Looks like Mercurial hair can be very deceptive to Moonbabies.'

Disguised or not, the motorhome didn't look to

Martha as if it had anything at all to do with space and it certainly wasn't dome shaped.

'They morph,' said Opal, reading her thoughts. 'They can change shape to suit their environment.' She held up a clump of wiry hair and patted the dried mud surface of the bonnet almost admiringly. 'The space-dome is one of the Mercurial clan's better inventions.'

'We need to get that bracelet off *now*,' said Martha, anxious to free Robbie of the Mercurial spell. She couldn't bear the idea of him staying with them for the whole night.

Opal sucked her teeth thoughtfully. 'Can't be done with fingers or scissors, or even knives,' she said. 'Mercurial hair's too zooming strong for that. When it's been woven anyway.'

'Exactly,' said Martha. 'So you'll have to get it off, Opal. You'll have to use your eye power.'

'What, now?' said Opal. She seemed hesitant, not like herself at all.

'Yes, now,' said Martha impatiently. 'Of course, now.'

Opal looked at her with large eyes.

'It's urgent!' Martha hissed.

'Righty dokey then.' Opal turned slowly to face Robbie, who was still muttering at his imaginary drivers, and fixed her eyes on the bracelet. Martha saw a few violet sparks fly out of Opal's eyes. They didn't fly very fast though and as soon as they made it through the windscreen they faded away. They didn't get anywhere near the bracelet.

'Stop messing about, Opal,' said Martha. 'We need to get this done.' She grabbed Opal's arm, trying to urge her on. 'What about the light-glances? And the dazzle-kicks?'

To Martha's horror, Opal let out a small wail. She'd never made a noise like that before. It sounded so helpless, it made Martha feel cold, and afraid.

'What is it? What's wrong?'

'Oh, Martha,' groaned Opal. 'I've been such a silly dummy brain-lame!'

Before Opal could explain what she meant, Martha put a hand over her mouth. She had heard a sound. The sound of a window opening further back in the motorhome. She pulled Opal quickly away into the shadows of the dustbins where they huddled together, keeping as still as possible.

Out of the corner of her eye, Martha saw the face at the open window. It was the same face she had seen before when the motorhome had almost run them over. Dark eyes gazed out of a swamp of hair. Brown and orange hair. Loads of it, crowding round the girl's face like a mass of angry scribbles drawn by a toddler. Only it wasn't a girl, Martha now realised. It was Perry. Peridot Mercurial.

'What was that noise, Peridot?'

Hearing Mineral's voice, Martha pressed herself against the dustbin as Peridot swung his head slowly from side to side, scanning the yard.

'It's nothing,' he said at last. 'Just Earth cats, fighting.'

'Good, then come here and give me my treatment.'

Peridot left the window and Martha dared to breathe again. 'No more noises,' she whispered in Opal's ear. Together they crept closer to the motorhome. Martha stood on tiptoe to see what was going on inside.

Mineral Mercurial was lying on a sunlounger wearing a cream bathrobe with a big green and orange brooch pinned to it. She looked quite different without her glasses and her face, with its extremely small nose and dark eyes, was almost identical to Peridot's. Her hair was even longer than his. It poured over the back of the lounger and streamed across the room, a raging river of black and brown and orange.

As Martha and Opal watched, Peridot squeezed an entire bottle of Luxury Locks onto his aunt's hair. Martha couldn't help wondering what Alesha would say if she saw that. Then Peridot picked the hair up very gently as if it was something precious, like the long train of a wedding dress, and began to rub the conditioner into it.

Mineral sighed contentedly. 'Ah, leastercalzz!'

'Oopsy, Auntie,' said Peridot, putting a finger to her lips. 'Remember what we said. No talking Carnelian on Earth. You don't mean leastercalzz. You mean lovely jubbly.'

'You're right,' answered Mineral. 'Yet I miss the old language. Never mind. We shall soon be home again.' She put a hand up to her brooch and stroked it. The brooch began to move. Its tongue flickered in and out and its tail, which was like a string of beads with a very sharp point at the end, waved restlessly up and down.

'Onyx!' Martha breathed. It wasn't a brooch. It was Mineral's mingle.

Until this time Garnet had stayed deep in Opal's cape pocket. Now he stretched up and put his tiny claws on the window. He made a chattering noise in his throat, the noise a cat makes when it sees a bird flying by, just out of reach. At the same moment, as if from nowhere, Beryl, Peridot's mingle, hit the inside of the window and stuck to it like a suction, her locust wings whirring aggressively.

Opal pressed a warning hand on Garnet's feathery head and he dropped down just as Peridot paused and looked towards the window. Luckily he was distracted by Robbie calling from the driver's cab. 'Come on, Perry-werry. We'll be hitting Brighton pier in a mo.'

'Hurry, Peridot,' said Mineral. 'The boy is waiting and you must finish my treatment. I want my hair to be at its very best. For tomorrow is a great day. Tomorrow we shall blot out a Moonbaby!' She rubbed her hands together and Peridot rubbed his together too, with conditioner.

'Evil lumps of space debris!' muttered Opal. 'I can see every word of what they're thinking. And it's not a pretty sight!'

'But why now?' whispered Martha. 'Why couldn't you see their thoughts before? Why didn't you know they were Mercurials straightaway?'

Opal pointed to the headscarf lying across Mineral's lap.

'That's why,' she said. 'They've found a way to camouflage their true identities with their headgear. That stuff blocks out my eyes the way your sun cream blocks out the sun. I can see them now though. Oh so very clearly. And I see they're no better than a blob of spat-out space-gum!'

'Everything is ready,' said Mineral. 'The web is in place, the challenge is set. You know what you have to do?'

'Of course I know, Auntie,' Peridot sneered. 'When you give the signal, Buttercup will go to the back of the stage, where you will be waiting. We will untie the cobweb and it will fall on the Moonbaby. The web will act like a vast sponge. It will absorb every drop of her power and she will be nothing but a husk. Useless, worthless and empty.' He sniggered. 'Everything will happen just as we agreed. It's going to be a very special night.'

'Good,' Mineral murmured. 'Very good. Then I shall look forward to telling that stuck up Bixbite Moonbaby that his pop-eyed little niece has lost her power and is living out the rest of her years on Planet Drabbar. Then we'll see who takes control of the Carnelian Coronet!'

'Yes,' simpered Peridot, beginning to wrap his hair in its usual elasticated hairnet. 'After tomorrow the Mercurial star will be in the ascendant. And the Moonbabies will begin their descent into nothingness.'

Mineral sat up. 'You're sure the boy won't stand in your way? When the time comes?'

'Quite sure. The blinding is secured to his arm. He'll do just what I tell him.'

'Yes,' said Mineral, taking something from her bathrobe pocket. 'He's quite your little pal now, isn't he? And we have such a lovely holiday snap of the two of you together in that ridiculous cow suit. This will show the rest of Carnelia that the Moonbabies aren't the only ones who can turn human beings into best friends.' She fanned her face with the photo. 'Shame the girl wouldn't accept her blinding though. Two friends would have been so much better than one. Two friends would have secured the Carnelian Coronet for us at once. Still, our bid remains strong enough.'

'That coronet will look so pretty-wetty on your hairy head,' said Peridot, winding a lock of Mineral's hair around his finger.

'Indeed, nephew,' crooned Mineral. 'Great days lie ahead. Great days! Mind you,' she said sharply. 'We'll have to keep an eye on that girl.'

Martha knew she meant her. The blindings she was talking about must be the bracelet Robbie was wearing, and the choker Mineral had tried to put round her neck.

'Don't worry, Auntie,' said Peridot. 'Robbie's sister Martha won't be able to do anything to stop us. No one can stop us now.'

He walked towards the window. Opal and Martha stepped back quickly. Peridot pulled Beryl off the glass with a squelch; he pressed her into his hairnet and went through the door to the driver's cab to join Robbie. Mineral reclined on her sunlounger, her eyes closed, a small smile playing on her mean little lips. No doubt she was imagining herself as Queen of Carnelia.

'The web is in place,' murmured Opal, still staring in at Mineral. 'The challenge is set.'

Martha took hold of Opal's arm. 'You have to break that cobweb, Opal. You have to destroy it. If you don't, the double dream will come true. They're going to drop it on you during the performance. They're going to cover you in their hair. From head to toe. They're going to rob you of all your power. You can't let them do it!'

Opal turned to her. 'Martha,' she said. 'There's zero I can do about it.'

'What?' Martha couldn't believe her ears. 'But the Mercurials are no match for a Moonbaby. You said so yourself. You can just turn your eyes up to maximum. You'll laser through that cobweb in an instant.'

'No,' Opal shook her head miserably. 'It's what I've been trying to tell you. I've let my eyes run down. I've been having so much fun at school, doing the play and everything, I forgot to take care of them. Oh, I've done the cucumbers and eyewash all right but I should have gone to Muckle Flugga lighthouse for a proper recharge. I should have gone ages ago. And now I haven't got the power to get there. You saw what happened just now. I couldn't even eye-break the puny little hair bracelet on Robbie's wrist. I've no power to combat that great cobweb. No power at all.'

Martha leaned on the side of the motorhome. She understood now why Opal's torch beams had been so dim on the way through the park. She understood too why Opal's eyes hadn't reacted to the flash from Mrs Underedge's camera. Opal's eyes were out of gas.

'Well then you mustn't go to the performance,' she said. 'We'll say you're sick. Just stay away from that cobweb and everything will be OK.'

Opal shook her head sadly. 'No. I have to go. I have to be at the performance.'

'That's ridiculous!' said Martha angrily. 'I know you love being on stage but it's not worth losing your powers and being exiled to Drabbar forever!'

'It's not that,' said Opal, staring straight ahead of her.

'What is it then?'

'It's the challenge. The challenge is set.' Opal spoke slowly and strangely, like a robot. Martha wanted to shake her.

'What do you mean? What challenge?' Why do you keep saying that?'

'The cobweb is a Mercurial challenge. I didn't see it coming and now it's been laid out before me. A Moonbaby can't turn her back on a Mercurial challenge.

If she does, she brings disgrace and humiliation on the entire Moonbaby clan. If I don't face the challenge, Uncle Bixbite will have to give up the Carnelian Coronet.'

Opal turned towards her. Martha couldn't see her face properly but she could make out the determined expression in her eyes. 'I don't care what happens to me,' said Opal, 'but I can't let Uncle Bixie be disgraced. I'd rather be sent to Drabbar for all eternity than let that happen. So I'll have to go. I'll go to the performance and when the cobweb falls, I will be underneath it.'

'No!' cried Martha. She'd already lost Opal once, twice if you counted the way they had fallen out. She couldn't lose her a third time and definitely not in this dreadful way. It was so cruel. It made her want to fight the Mercurials herself. She'd tear their hair out with her bare hands if only she could. 'No!' she said again.

'Yes,' said Opal. She smiled through the dark. 'It's the only way, dear friend.'

Martha felt so helpless, it was agony. She let herself slide down the side of the motorhome until she was crouching in potholes of engine oil and rainwater. Opal slid down beside her. She was very still and calm, as if she had already accepted her fate. Martha linked an arm through hers.

'We can't give up now,' she said. 'There must be something we can do.'

'There's nothing,' said Opal. 'The Mercurials are the winners. I took my eye off the bauble, Martha, and I'll have to take the consequences.'

They were silent for a moment, both of them imagining what it would be like when the cobweb dropped onto Opal the following night.

'Will it hurt very much?' said Martha. 'Are you scared?'

Opal shook her head. 'Not me. I'm a big alien now, you know. I'm not scared. Not one megabyte. I'll miss Carnelia though, and Earth.' Her voice dropped to an even quieter whisper as she added, 'And all my favourite Earthlings, of course.'

Garnet began spinning his head round and round in anguish. 'We'll both miss them, won't we, Garnie?' Opal patted him until he settled down in her arms.

'I'll miss Uncle Bixie too,' she said. 'I would have liked to tell him what a wise old uncle he's been to me. I won't get the chance now.'

Opal lifted her head and Martha looked into her eyes. There was no fear in them, but they were full of difficult thoughts, decisions and sadness.

'You're very brave,' she said, turning away from her friend and racking her brains again for some idea of how to help her. Part of her wanted to tell Opal how she would feel, how much she would miss her when she was gone but that would be admitting defeat and even though Opal seemed to have accepted that her future would be spent on Drabbar, Martha wasn't ready to do that yet. But what could she do? *What?*

Water dripped out of a pipe somewhere high on the bus depot wall. Martha shivered and put her hands in her pockets. One of them held Robbie's chocolate raisin box. She turned it over in her hand. Then she turned it over again. And again.

'What if,' she said slowly. 'What if something interfered with the Mercurials? What if something distracted them? Could you get away then, do you think?'

'Perhaps,' said Opal. 'It'd have to be something extremely major though.'

Martha felt a scheme beginning to hatch in her brain. 'The Mercurials really care about their hair, don't they?' she said.

Opal nodded. 'The way human beings care about their mobile phones and newborn babies.'

'So they wouldn't like it then, if anything . . . funny happened to it. If anything sort of . . . messed with it?'

'They'd hate it. They like their hair to be span and spick. I mean, spack and spin.'

'Spick and span.'

'That too,' Opal agreed.

'I have an idea,' said Martha.

'I can see it,' said Opal, looking at her gravely. 'And I think it might work. There might just be time. Are you quite sure you want to go through with it?'

Martha swallowed. 'Yes,' she said. 'I'm sure.' She stood up.

'I'll be right out here, waiting,' said Opal. 'If you need me, just holler your head off and I'll be in there faster than you can say Jack Higginson.'

Martha didn't have to explain the plan to Opal. Opal had read her mind and knew what she was about to do. It felt good, Opal being in her mind again. Having her there, deep in her thoughts, made Martha feel a lot braver than she would have done otherwise.

She walked to the back of the motorhome and tapped on the door.

Chapter Twenty-three

Instantly there was a commotion from inside. Martha heard the springs of the sunlounger squeak. Then there was a sweeping sound that Martha took to be hair, great batches of it, being dragged along the floor. After that she couldn't hear anything for a while and she thought Mineral must be bundling up her hair, stashing it away out of sight. Martha wished they would hurry up and answer the door. The longer she stood there, the more she wanted to change her mind and run away.

At last the door opened and Mineral appeared, putting on her glasses. 'Who is it?' she began crossly. ' What do you want at this time of—' She broke off, stopped and smiled. 'Oh, it's you, sweetie-pudding,' she said. 'What can I do for you, my dear?'

'I . . . I . . .' Martha couldn't make any words come out at first but she forced herself to go on. 'I've had a bit of a re-think,' she said. 'I was wondering . . .'

'Ye-es,' encouraged Mineral. 'What were you wondering?'

'Whether . . . if . . . I mean, do you still have that choker? I thought maybe . . . I would like it after all. If .

.. if it's OK with you, that is.'

Mineral opened the door wider. 'OK?' she tinkled a strange and hollow laugh. 'Of course it's OK. It's more than OK. I have it right here as a matter of factly.' She took it out of her bathrobe pocket. 'I'll put it on for you, shall I?'

She reached out towards Martha's neck but Martha said, 'No, it's all right. I'll put it on later. I'd like to look at it for a bit first. It's so . . . so pretty.' She knew that if the choker really fastened itself around her neck she would be just like Robbie, no longer able to see the Mercurials for what they were. She would be no use to Opal like that.

'Very well.' Mineral sniffed. 'As you wish.' Then one corner of her mouth turned up with pleasure. 'I'm sure it will look lovely on, as lovely as a coronet!'

'Mmm,' Martha murmured, trying to return Mineral's smile. Her face felt frozen. Now came the most difficult part. She gripped the raisin box in her pocket. It was her fervent hope that Mark and Kevin and Clive were still alive, and that at least one of them was a girl. A pregnant girl. Feeling for the lid she began to fumble open the flaps but it was tricky to do with the fingers of only one hand. It was taking too long.

'Was there anything else?' asked Mineral. 'Because I have some weaving to do.' She already seemed anxious for Martha to leave.

'It's very kind of you,' said Martha, flicking back the second flap with her index finger. 'Would it . . . would it be all right if I gave you a hug?'

'A hug?' said Mineral. 'Why, yes, I don't see why not. We're friends now, after all. Aren't we, Martha?' She held out her arms, ready to receive Martha into her embrace.

'Yes. We are.' Martha gritted her teeth and leaned forward. As Mineral's hands rested on her back, she reached up around her neck. With one hand she felt for the edge of the orange headwrap, lifting it slightly until her fingers met a clump of wiry hair. With the other hand she shook the little box, trying to empty it into Mineral's hairline. She didn't have more than a moment. She couldn't even see what she was doing. She just prayed that the lice had seen the new home she was offering them and had gone on in.

'Goodnight, then,' said Mineral, straightening up.

Martha wrapped her hand round the raisin box and quickly put it behind her back.

'Goodnight,' she said. 'And thank you.'

Mineral turned to go in but then she paused and said, 'See you at the performance, sugar-heart.' She clapped her hands together. 'And what a performance it will be!'

She closed the door behind her, leaving Martha shaking like a leaf in the dark.

Opal appeared at once. 'Great work!' she whispered, patting her arm.

'But *will* it work?' Martha whispered back.

'It will,' said Opal. 'Mark's a boy, but Kevin and Clive are girls all right. Once those little creatures get into Mercurial hair, they'll breed like everybody's business. They're going to spread like, like . . .'

'Wildfire?' suggested Martha.

'Exactly,' said Opal. 'They'll spread like wildfire.'

'I just hope they can do it quickly enough,' Martha said with a shiver.

Opal put her arm around her. 'You're frosting!' she

204

said. 'Let's get you back to the Domestipod. We'll soon have you warm as roast.'

As they walked away, Martha looked back at the motorhome. Robbie and Peridot were in the driving seat together now. Robbie was jamming the gears into place and chatting happily.

Poor Robbie. He didn't have any idea who he was with or what was about to happen. And Martha couldn't do anything about it, not until she could figure out a way to release him from that bracelet. She lifted a hand and gave him a brief wave, a wave she knew he couldn't see.

As the two girls made their way back through the darkness of the park, their purple capes wrapped around them, Martha felt full of fear for Opal and Robbie. She felt so responsible for what happened next, it was as if she was practically an adult. She was still a ten-year-old girl but she didn't feel like one. She felt like someone else entirely.

The Domestipod welcomed them back with warm air and calming music. There was even cocoa waiting for them in the scoff capsule dispenser. When they had drunk it, the Domestipod flung out Opal's hammock and a second hammock for Martha so that they could sleep right next to each other. Garnet settled down in his own little hammock beneath theirs. He sniffed it a bit, then turned round three times, let out a sigh and went to sleep.

Opal lay on her side in her hammock facing Martha.

'I think I've been missing you, Martha.'

Martha knew all about missing people. She had missed Opal so much that her chest ached. She didn't say that though. She said, 'Why would you miss me? I've been here all the time.'

'I know you have, but I haven't. Not in my head anyway. I've been away with the pixies.'

'Fairies,' said Martha, lying on her back and staring up at the crescent moon light shade.

Opal nodded. 'Yes. I've been away with the pixies and the elves and the fairies too. I've been away with the lot of them.'

'But you're back now, aren't you?'

'Yes I am,' said Opal.

'I just hope those head lice are getting to work,' said Martha, biting her lip.

'Don't fret, Martha,' said Opal. She reached across and took Martha's hand. 'They are getting to work. Mark and Kevin and Clive think they're in paradise. They think they've died and gone to seventieth heaven. Those little head lice will be biting holes in Mineral's scalp right now. And tomorrow, they'll be having babies by the billion.'

'I hope you're right,' said Martha. 'I hope we'll be in time.'

'Of course we'll be in time,' murmured Opal drowsily. 'And if we're not, well, I've got another little scheme up my trouser leg.'

'Have you?' asked Martha. 'What sort of scheme?'

But Opal was already snoring.

Martha stared up at the ceiling or a while, thinking of Robbie and hoping he was all right, but soon she too began to fall asleep.

The two girls lay suspended in their hammocks, swaying slightly, still holding hands. They stayed like that until morning.

Chapter Twenty-four

The next day passed all too quickly. Before she knew it, Martha was strapping her harp costume on her back and climbing up to her place on the giant's table. The heavy blue curtains at the front of the stage were closed but Martha could hear the loud hum of the audience, all chatting away, eager for the show to start. Mum was out there somewhere, in among all the other parents and families. Martha swallowed nervously, wondering just what sort of show they were about to see.

The other members of the cast were giggling excitedly and giving each other good-luck signals. Martha kept glancing at Opal who was squatting quietly in her starting position as the beanstalk. She looked still and serene. How could she be so calm? Martha was so agitated she couldn't keep her legs from jiggling up and down.

'Nervous?' said Jessie.

'Very,' said Martha. She couldn't tell Jessie just how nervous though. Or why.

'Don't worry,' said Jessie. 'Stage fright goes away once the performance starts. That's what my granny says.'

Martha nodded. She wasn't reassured but she tried to

look as if she was, because Jessie was being kind. Her heart leaped as she saw Buttercup ambling onto the stage, Robbie and Peridot inside. At least Robbie had survived the night in the motorhome but he was still in Peridot's power and he still had no idea what was going on.

'By the way,' said Jessie. 'I've been meaning to ask. Can you come to my house tomorrow? It's my birthday. I'm going to the cinema and Gran says I'm allowed to bring a friend.' She gave Martha a hand-drawn invitation.

'What?' Martha was distracted. She hadn't even known Jessie's birthday was coming up.

'Sorry,' said Jessie. 'It's a silly time to give it to you, and it's ever such short notice, but I didn't want to forget.'

Martha recognised the drawing on the invitation. She had seen Jessie doing it during the quiet spells in rehearsals. She had spent ages on it. 'Thanks,' she said, remembering her manners.

'That's OK.' Jessie smiled. 'I hope you can make it.'

Martha realised suddenly how much she liked Jessie. She was so thoughtful. She was never unkind to anyone, and she was very friendly too, in her own quiet way.

'Of course I'll come,' said Martha. 'I'd love to. I'll ask Mum tonight.' She folded the invitation and, since she didn't have a pocket in her costume, tucked it into the top of her leggings instead.

'Great,' said Jessie.

'Can't wait,' said Martha. Then she turned and saw the giant cobweb. She forgot about Jessie and her party immediately.

The cobweb looked more menacing than ever. Its dark centre stood out from the backdrop, pushing towards the main stage. It seemed to be throbbing like a living thing and straining at its fixings as if it knew what its task was, as if it was ready to strike.

Martha was even more alarmed by the sight of Mineral Mercurial lurking at the back of the stage. She was standing right by a rope that trailed at the side of the cobweb. There was a similar rope dangling at the other side of the stage, Martha saw. That must be the one Peridot was supposed to pull, to bring the cobweb down on Opal.

The worst thing about Mineral was that she looked just as she always did. Her headwrap was tied smoothly around her hair. She was quite unruffled, not a bit like someone with a severe case of nits and head lice. She caught Martha's eye and nodded at her. There was one thing new about her after all; the look of evil triumph that glittered in her eyes. Martha made herself nod back. As she did, she instinctively put a hand to her throat. She wasn't wearing the choker and she had done her shirt buttons up right to the top so that Mineral couldn't tell she wasn't really in her power. She forced herself to smile at her, the way she would smile at someone she genuinely liked. Mineral smiled back, a satisfied smile.

A thin curtain separated Martha and Jessie from the front of the stage. Their scene wasn't until later when Jack reached the giant's castle in the clouds. They were meant to sit quietly in the darkness until then.

Opal also had to wait. Martha could see her through the flimsy curtain. She was keeping low in her beanstalk enclosure, behind the stepladder, waiting until she was supposed to start growing.

Mrs Underedge, who had been on edge all day, stood by the props table, gripping the script with both hands, as if she thought it might fly away otherwise.

'Absolutely still, everyone,' she hissed. 'Now. *Overture!*' She pressed a button and the opening music began. The lights came up on the front of the stage and the main curtains jerked open.

Chloe, who was playing Jack's mother, had the first lines. She told Jack, who was really Tom Barnes, to go to market and sell their cow. They were so poor, she said, that they would have to sell their beloved Buttercup.

Buttercup, who was meant to stand patiently during this scene, was behaving in a very unusual way. She appeared to be doing an odd little dance. She'd never done that in rehearsals. Martha suspected it was because Peridot, who was the front end of the cow, was trying to head to the back of the stage towards the cobweb, while Robbie, the back end, was trying to head in the other direction to their usual place at the front of the stage. The result was that Buttercup looked rather unsteady on her four legs. She kept toppling to one side and then to the other. The audience started to titter.

Chloe began to giggle too but Tom was quite put out. He liked acting and was proud of having the main part in the play. He probably thought the boys inside the cow were showing off or trying to upstage him. While he said his lines, which were all about how much he loved Buttercup, he kept elbowing her crossly, trying to get her to stand still. That made the audience chuckle all the more.

Then it was time for the dance of the five magic beans and for Opal to begin to grow. Buttercup was supposed to be off stage by now, but she wasn't. She was jerking in all directions as Peridot tried to manoeuvre himself towards his side of the cobweb, and as Robbie did his best to leave the stage as they were supposed to. Worryingly, Peridot seemed to be winning the battle and Buttercup was getting far too close to the cobweb for Martha's liking. She could see the hungry gleam in Mineral's dark eyes as Peridot edged closer to his desired position.

Now Opal was starting to grow. She was bravely climbing her little ladder and hooking on her green leaves as she went. She couldn't see what was going on behind her, or that Peridot and Mineral both had hold of their ropes now, but she must know. She must know that the cobweb was about to drop on her at any moment.

Martha was in despair. Why wasn't Mineral's head itching? What were Mark and Kevin and Clive playing at? She couldn't bear it. She wanted to warn Opal, to make her get out of the way. She couldn't though, because Opal had already resolved to go through with this. She had to; the challenge was set.

Yet Martha couldn't just sit by and do nothing. She wanted to show Opal that she knew what was going through her mind, that they were in this together. They were a team. She couldn't say all that out loud so she did the only other thing she could think of. She started to sing.

'No need to be sad, Sir,
No need for you to frown.'

'What are you doing, Martha?' Jessie whispered. 'It's not our scene for ages.'

Martha couldn't answer. She just opened her hands apologetically and went on singing.

'No need to be down, Sir,
Not when I'm around.'

'Not yet!' hissed Mrs Underedge, making urgent cutting gestures across her throat. *'Not yet!'* Poor Mrs Underedge. She had nagged and nagged at Martha not to come in late with the song, and now she was coming in way too early. But somehow she couldn't stop. She was singing to Opal. It was her message to Opal, maybe the last message she would ever be able to send her.

'I will sing to you, Sir,
Lift your heart up high.
I will sing to you, Sir,
Raise your spirits to the sky.'

Opal turned then and smiled at her. She must have been able to see the Mercurials, tugging at the ropes that held the cobweb, but she didn't make any attempt to jump out of the way. The cobweb was going to drop on her at any moment. The head lice weren't doing their job at all. Martha's plan had failed. If she hadn't been so frightened she could have cried. Instead, she just carried on singing. As she sang she stared at Opal. She couldn't take her eyes off her. She was trying to memorise everything about her: her hair, her gangly body, her pointed ears, her strange and beautiful eyes. She needed to file it all away into her memory before it was too late. Martha realised, her voice faltering on the long notes, that she was singing a goodbye song; the song was a message of farewell to her wonderful alien friend.

She finished singing and slumped down on the table. The weight of her harp costume suddenly felt overwhelming.

But Opal didn't look perturbed. She winked at Martha, then turned to the front again and carried on climbing her ladder and unfurling her leaves. When she reached the top, she started speaking, which was a big surprise for everyone, because the beanstalk didn't have any lines.

'Hello, ladies and gentlemenfolk,' she said, addressing the audience in a loud voice. 'I bet you've never seen a beanstalk like me before, have you? Aren't you going to take some photos? I'm the Eighth Wonder of the World, I am. I'm the new Statue of Flibbertigibbets. I'm the Knickeragara Falls. I'm Mount Ever-rested. You should get a snap of me so you can show it to your grandchildren. Come on, everybody. Get your digital whatnots out and I'll stand very still while you fire off some shots. Don't forget to flash!' She struck a dramatic pose and waited.

'Opal!' Mrs Underedge cried from the wings. 'Opal Moonbaby! What in the world are you *doing*?'

Opal didn't change position. 'Sorry, Mrs U,' she said over her shoulder. 'Just didn't want to miss the photo opportunity. But don't worry, normal service will be resumed ASAS. As Soon As Sensible!' she proclaimed dramatically, like an old and magnificent actor.

The audience started laughing again and taking out their cameras and mobile phones and pointing them at Opal. Hundreds of flashes went off. Little white lights flickered and danced around the hall. Suddenly Martha realised what Opal was up to. She was soaking up all the flashes with her eyes, trying to bring the power back to them. Martha drew herself upright, a tiny nugget of hope beginning to grow in her chest.

Most people's eyes were fixed on Opal now but Martha kept glancing round to see what the Mercurials were up to. Mineral and Peridot were trying to release the cobweb ropes but the one at Peridot's side kept sticking. Buttercup held the rope in her teeth and was tugging at it but the cobweb wouldn't fall.

Then Martha saw Onyx, Mineral's mingle, slide from his mistress's headwrap and into the cobweb. He began to weave his way diagonally across it towards the hook that held the web on Peridot's side. Next Martha saw something being ejected from Buttercup's mouth. Not a gobbet of chewed grass as you might expect from a cow's mouth but a squishy slimy thing, like a used hanky. It was Beryl. She clung onto the cobweb and began to inch upwards towards the hook on Peridot's side. It was taking her an age, Martha was relieved to see, but then Beryl produced her wings and with a whir took off and landed straight on the hook. At once she began to work the web free. She must have sharp locust teeth as well as wings because the web started to give way immediately and it would have been down on Opal in seconds ... if Beryl hadn't suddenly been attacked by a flying rabbit.

Garnet!

Martha hadn't been the only one watching the Mercurial mingles' progress towards the hook. Garnet pinned Beryl down with one paw and swiped at the approaching Onyx with the other. But Onyx slithered along undaunted, flickering his tongue as he went.

'Look out, Garnie!' Martha said. He would never be able to fight the two of them off at once.

The audience finished taking photographs of Opal and there was a pause. No one knew how to get the play back on track. No one knew where they were in the script any more so they all started saying their lines at once. The magic beans, who had already done their dance once, did it all over again, Colette clucked and flapped about madly, Tom started putting on his climbing gear, Ravi began fee-fi-fo-fumming and Jessie banged her rolling pin on the table. Buttercup and Mineral Mercurial were still tugging angrily at the cobweb's ropes and shouting instructions at one another's mingles.

Mrs Underedge had her head in her hands and was crying out in anguish. 'Stop this . . . *cacophony*. Stop this . . . this . . . *pandemonium*. Stop it at once! Oh! I'll be the laughing stock of the staffroom!'

The audience were in fits of laughter. They had expected a performance of the traditional *Jack and the Beanstalk* story. This new version was much more entertaining.

It was about to become more entertaining still.

Opal raised her hands slowly and leaned her head way back until she was looking at the ceiling. She appeared to be in a deep trance.

Following Opal's gaze, Martha saw two oval light beams fix themselves on the flaking paintwork of the ceiling. She caught her breath as she realised the lights, which were violet and eye-shaped, were beginning to sparkle and to grow. More colours appeared in them and began to swirl in the violet background, turquoise following silver, green chasing after gold. Martha knew that these growing light beams were the reflections of Opal's true eyes. She had seen Opal's real eyes just once before. It was a camera flash that had revealed them that time too. They were huge, with many shimmering colours, always moving and full of flickering light.

As the reflections from her eyes reached their full size,

Opal raised her hands like two big stop signs. Everything came to a halt. The magic beans stopped dancing, Tom stopped climbing the Opal beanstalk and Jessie stopped banging her rolling pin on the table. Ravi stopped fi-fi-fo-fumming, Colette stopped clucking and the Mercurials stood absolutely still.

Martha heard a fizzing sound, like a rocket soaring into the sky. Suddenly the room lit up. Not just the stage but the entire school hall. There was a bang and a blinding white light filled the room, then flashed violet, then indigo, then purple and dazzling white again. A mass of silver stars began to circle just beneath the ceiling. Opal motioned at the stars with her hands and they shot off in all directions. The stars dived and twisted and somersaulted and loop-the-looped in a high-speed sky dance, like silver jets at an air display. Opal stood in the middle of the stage directing the stars with her hands as if she was a famous conductor leading an orchestra.

The audience and the cast stared up at the glittering stars, open-mouthed. Martha stared at them too and felt herself beginning to smile. 'Go for it, Opal,' Martha murmured. 'Go for it!'

Opal flicked out a foot, and a set of stars streaked across the stage. They flashed past Martha's face and headed straight for Buttercup, disappearing right up her nose. 'So *that's* what a dazzle-kick looks like!' Martha whispered.

Opal made a karate chop with her arm and another set of stars soared over Martha's head at astonishing speed. There was a crackle like the searing sound of oil hitting a wet frying pan. Martha thought that one must be a light laser. Opal really could do all the things she had boasted about. Martha was trembling with excitement now. Maybe this wasn't the last day Opal would ever spend on Earth.

For a second everything went dark and then a single light came up, shining on the cobweb. Every evil strand was illuminated, each shade of orange and brown and black perfectly defined. The rest of the stage was cloaked in gloom but Martha could just make out the silhouette of Opal on her ladder, the runner-bean flower on her head shimmering a little. Opal made a pulling action with one hand and Garnet, who was still grappling valiantly with Beryl, let go of her and dropped to the giant's table. He came and sat on Martha's legs, and made excited *chi-chi-chi* noises.

The cobweb began to glow, brighter and brighter until it looked as though it was on fire. Then, it began to turn. It began to spin. Faster and faster it went, whisking round and round. The most enormous Catherine Wheel in the world. It made Martha dizzy just to look at it. She wondered how Onyx and Beryl were feeling. They were still in the web somewhere, no doubt clinging to it for dear life.

Mineral rushed round in front of the cobweb. She tried to catch it and stop it from spinning but each time she touched it the cobweb went into reverse and spun in the other direction. It was completely out of her control. Then it started to spin even more violently, faster, furiously, like a washing machine in full spin. It began to move forward in thin air. Nothing was holding it any longer. It was travelling all by itself. Did Opal have control of the cobweb now? Was her eye power going to be strong enough to fight the Mercurials and their mingles?

Mineral Mercurial stepped backwards and yelled at the cobweb.

'No,' she screamed. 'Go back! Stop! Stop, I say! Deeaxxebblyzz! Frantazz!'

She covered her head with her hands as the cobweb suddenly seemed to obey her and stopped spinning. The light went straight out of it and it fell forward onto Mineral. She collapsed to the ground, swamped by its hairy weight. Mineral was caught. Caught in her own horrible trap.

The audience gasped. So did the cast.

Then a voice said, 'Phoooooaaaaaaarr! Perry, you don't half stink, you know! Don't you ever have a bath?'

The lights came up on the stage and Martha saw Robbie and Peridot both sitting up in the Buttercup costume. Peridot was staring aghast at his aunt. Robbie, was standing up and shaking something off his wrist. The hairy bracelet was broken and he was free of it at last. Robbie dropped it to the floor and Martha saw a few silver stars fall and bounce on top of it.

'I'm off!' announced Robbie. 'I don't care what anyone says. I can't stand another second in this costume. It's imploding and disintegrating. It smells like a billion random farts have gone off in it!'

It was the old Robbie, back to his usual self.

The audience started tittering again and Martha laughed too. The audience were laughing because they thought it was funny. Martha was laughing with relief.

Then a fearful wail went up. The blood-curdling cry rose over all the other noise, stamping it out.

Mineral Mercurial staggered to her feet, still inside the cobweb. She lurched forward, dragging the web with her. She tore at it with her hands, trying to find a way out. At last she appeared from underneath, tugging wildly at her hair and unwinding her long orange headwrap. Her hair streamed out in all directions as she shook her head from side to side. Her hair was a flying forest of black and orange corkscrews and Martha saw that it matched the cobweb exactly.

Mrs Underedge, meanwhile, at a loss as to how to regain control, was hammering away at the music, skipping from track to track, trying to begin the first scene again.

Mineral clutched at her head, and cried out, 'What is this prickling, this tickling, this crawling? Oh, the itch! A plague! A plague! A terribly terrible lurgy!'

It was working! Martha's plan had been a good one after all.

'Oh, prickling! Oh, tickling! Oh, crawling!' ranted Mineral. 'Prickling! Tickling! Crawling!' She whirled her hair round and round. The audience began clapping along to the music, convinced they were watching some brand new and outlandish dance.

Mineral swayed around the stage, moaning and crying. Peridot shuffled behind her in the now limp Buttercup costume. He was pulling off his hairnet and scratching frantically at his scalp. The head lice must have found their way into his hair too. He flung his arms around Mineral's waist and the two of them fought their way to the wings and staggered from the stage.

As the Mercurials fled, all the lights and stars fizzed and popped and then went out entirely. Opal twisted in her beanstalk enclosure and bent over double. Martha could see she was exhausted but the audience took the bend for a bow; they got to their feet immediately, clapping madly. The clapping seemed to revive Opal and she smiled out at the audience and waved. She turned to Martha and waved to her too. Martha waved back and saw that Opal's eyes had returned to their usual size. The clapping going on around them was incredibly loud but Martha and Opal barely noticed it. Together they had foiled the Mercurials' horrible scheme and they knew it. They had won.

Mrs Underedge blundered onto the stage holding the fire extinguisher, pointing it in all directions, looking for the source of the fire. She was so alarmed she hadn't noticed the clapping. She looked completely flummoxed as Miss Brocklebank came rushing up the steps and shook her hand and hugged her, fire extinguisher and all.

'Marvellous, Monica!' Miss Brocklebank exclaimed. 'What a superb show! I never knew you had it in you. Comedy, lighting, whirling dervishes. The lot. Congratulations! That was the best school play we've ever had! I do hope you'll direct again for us next year.'

Mrs Underedge adjusted her glasses. 'Well, I . . . don't really . . . that is—' She didn't need to finish her sentence because one of the infants came up on stage and gave her a big bunch of flowers and Miss Brocklebank asked her to take a bow. A rare smile twitched at the corners of Mrs Underedge's mouth. She took a bow, and Opal and Martha bowed with her.

Chapter Twenty-five

Martha skipped back from the mini-market, swinging her shopping bag and singing her harp song at the top of her voice. She had slept really well for the first time in ages, and had woken from a wonderful dream which had got the day off to a brilliant start. She had been feeling blissfully happy all morning.

Opal and Robbie were sitting where she'd left them, on the pipe in the play area. She hopped up to join them and passed round crisps and cartons of juice from her bag.

'They haven't come out yet, then?' she said, seeing the Mercurial motorhome still blocking the pavement. Mineral and Peridot had arrived at the salon first thing, banging on the door, begging to have their hair cut off. Mum was giving them the Big T. It was taking her ages to cut off all that hair.

'No, you haven't missed anything,' said Robbie. 'Any minute now, though.'

'Yes,' said Opal, looking right into the salon. 'Marie Stephens has just put the clippers on the final setting.'

Martha was surprised she could see so far. She thought

she must have used up all her new eye power the night before. 'Are you feeling OK today, Opal?' she asked, checking her over.

'Oh, I'm fine,' said Opal. 'Right as reindeer. The audience took so many photos of me I'm quite well topped up, thank you for asking.'

'But what about those photos?' said Martha. Something was still worrying her. 'Remember in the summer, when you took that photo of yourself with Mum's mobile phone? Your real eyes were in the picture.'

'Yes,' said Robbie. 'I remember that. You looked like an actual alien in that one.'

'I am an actual alien,' said Opal, popping open her crisp packet.

'But we had to delete that photo straightaway,' said Martha. 'Won't everyone in the audience have a photo of your alien eyes now?'

'No,' said Opal. 'I kept my eyes closed while I soaked up their snap power. The audience will have pictures of me with my eyes shut. I expect they'll think I was just having a little nappy.'

'Nap!' said Martha and Robbie together.

'Whatever you say,' said Opal, munching a crisp. 'Anyway, the point is, my secret is safe as trousers.'

'Houses!' said Robbie and Martha, both dissolving into giggles.

'Yes, if you like. In any case, the really good news is I've got enough eye power left to get to Muckle Flugga so I'm still on course to get my CIA.'

'Muckle Flugga,' said Martha, rolling the words around her mouth. 'I love that name.' She remembered something then and said slowly, 'I love the island too.'

'So do I,' said Robbie in a voice that was unusually dreamy for him.

Martha looked at him. 'Really?'

'Really. It's got the most awesome lighthouse ever.'

'What's the lighthouse like?' said Martha, a realisation beginning to dawn on her.

'White, with a massive light on top.'

'And what else?'

'Amazing rock pools,' said Robbie.

'Loads of sea anemones?'

'And thousands of hermit crabs.'

'Cold water, though.'

'Freezing water,' Robbie agreed. Then he stared at her, as the realisation began to dawn on him too.

'Funny puffins?' said Martha.

Robbie nodded. 'Very funny puffins. And it's got the most fantastic, brilliant, random, immense—'

'Sunsets!' Martha finished.

'Sunsets!' repeated Robbie and he lifted his hand in the air. 'High five!'

Martha slapped her palm against his. She couldn't stop smiling at the thought that they'd had another double dream.

'That's Muckle Flugga, all right,' said Opal. 'That's the place, exactly. Hey! I thought you two said you'd never been there.'

'We haven't,' said Martha.

'Not exactly,' said Robbie.

'Not yet, anyway,' Martha added with a grin.

'Oh, I see!' said Opal, understanding. 'It's like that is it? It was supposed to be a surprise, but I might as well tell you, since you seem to know already.'

Before she could say more, the bell on the salon door jangled sharply and Mineral and Peridot tottered out. They were completely bald. The wintry breeze that met their naked scalps made them shiver and grimace as they rushed to the motorhome and struggled up into the driver's cab.

Mineral revved the engine and the motorhome lurched, and then reversed off the pavement. With a crash of gears, it screeched away down the road, fumes billowing from its exhaust.

'Their power's all gone now,' Martha said, watching as the Mercurials' motorhome took a left and disappeared round the corner.

'Yes,' said Opal. 'Thanks to you.'

'And you,' Martha reminded her. 'My plan didn't work in time. It was your eye power that did it really.'

'And Mark and Kevin and Clive, don't forget,' put in Robbie.

'Yes,' said Martha. She was feeling a bit guilty about Mark and Kevin and Clive. 'I'm sorry we had to sacrifice them, Robbie. I hope you don't mind too much.'

Robbie nodded solemnly. 'You had to do what you had to do,' he said. 'You had to save Opal. And anyway, I'm glad. I can't believe I was going around saying that smelly Mercurial creep was nice. People must have thought my mind was imploding.'

They were distracted by a huge roaring sound, coming from behind the park.

'Look!' cried Martha. 'Look there!'

A massive dark brown dome lumbered over the trees, steam spurting from its base. It began to rise higher, over the houses, over the flats and up towards the clouds.

'The Mercurials' space-dome,' said Opal.

'It looks more like a dirty flowerpot to me,' said Robbie.

'Where do you think they're going?' asked Martha. 'Back to Carnelia?'

'Shouldn't think so,' said Opal. 'They won't want to show themselves there with those doorknob heads. They'll need to find somewhere quiet to grow their hair back and pick their wounds. But the main thing is they've gone. And they won't be bothering us again.' She stood on the pipe and waved at the dome as it disappeared into a large cloud. 'Good riddance to bad radishes!' she yelled. Then she ran up and down the pipe whooping.

Martha promptly picked up her shopping bag so that Opal wouldn't accidentally tread on it as she danced and cackled her way along the pipe. It was good to see Opal bouncing around again. Martha had seen a new, much more serious side to her friend over the last couple of days. Opal had acted so bravely. She had behaved as if *she* didn't matter at all; her only thought had been to protect her uncle and to keep the good name of the Moonbabies. She had been daring and brilliant. Martha could see now why Opal was such a strong contender for the Carnelian Coronet. She would definitely get Martha's vote, if she had one. Opal was easily distracted and had a tendency to get carried away but in the end she was unselfish, fearless and loyal. There was no one quite like her. Martha felt very proud to be her friend.

Opal grew tired of dancing and sat down next to Martha. She put her arm round her, her violet eyes gleaming with pleasure. 'Now,' she said. 'I'm taking you two on a trip!'

'I knew it,' said Robbie, leaping onto the pipe beside Opal. 'I can't wait. This is it. This is going to be so immense!'

Behind them, the Domestipod glowed pink and purple and Garnet spun his head round in a circle, eager to be off.

'Oh, not today, though,' cried Martha in dismay. 'I'm really sorry but I can't go today. I'm doing something else.'

'What?' said Opal, her mouth dropping open in horror. 'You can't be!'

'What are you on about, Martha?' Robbie demanded. 'You know this is meant to happen. We both do. We double dreamed it. We've got proof!'

'Sorry,' Martha said again. She hated having to disappoint them both. 'It was a fantastic dream, Robbie,' she said. 'And I'm not ignoring it. Honestly I'm not.'

She turned to Opal. 'And I know you can make our dream come true, Opal, but the thing is, I've been invited on Jessie's birthday outing. It's today. I'm meeting her and her gran at the bus-stop in half an hour.'

'But this is way more important,' said Robbie. 'You'll have to make an excuse. Tell Jessie you've broken both your legs. Say they've disintegrated and you won't be able to get on the bus.'

'I can't do that. I promised Jessie I'd be there.' Martha patted the shopping bag. 'I've bought her a present and everything.' She paused for a moment before adding, 'And anyway, I *want* to go.'

It was true. Martha felt really pleased that Jessie had chosen her to come on her birthday outing. She was looking forward to it and she was planning to invite Jessie over to her flat one day too. She was even thinking of asking Jessie to be her partner when they had to pair up and make models for their solar system projects. Jessie was a good friend, and Martha wanted to spend time with her.

Suddenly Opal fell backwards off the pipe and landed flat on her back on the hard ground. She lay there clutching her stomach and groaning. Martha jumped down after her immediately.

'What is it? What's the matter?'

Opal writhed around and moaned, her eyes squeezed shut.

'Are you in agony?' said Robbie. 'Is it an alien illness? Are you going to implode?'

Opal opened one eye. 'Awful pangs!' she said.

'Pangs?' asked Martha.

'Yes,' Opal nodded, 'Earth pangs. Pangs of jealousy.'

'Jealousy?' Martha was puzzled. 'What are you jealous of?'

'Jessie!' wailed Opal, rubbing her stomach and her chest. 'I can't bear it that you're going to spend the afternoon with her instead of me. It's giving me terrible jealousy. It feels awful. I hate jealousy. It hurts. It's not a bit like a pudding! Ow! Ow, ow!' She began to roll around again.

'Well, at least you'll be able to describe how it feels,' said Robbie, 'when you're writing the Human Handybook, I mean.'

'No,' said Opal, hugging her knees. 'The Human Handybook's full. I've run out of space.'

'That reminds me,' said Martha. She opened her bag and brought out a large notebook with lots of pages of lined paper. 'I bought a present for you too, Opal.'

Opal sat up, the pangs of jealousy instantly forgotten. 'For me?' she said. 'You bought a present for me?'

'Yes,' answered Martha. 'Since you're going to be here for a while yet, I thought you might want to have another go at writing the Human Handybook. In case you thought you'd missed anything out of the first one.'

Opal took the fat notebook from Martha and cuddled it. 'I missed out a lot,' she said. 'I missed out remembering who your friends are and not getting carried away by new ones. I missed out loyalty too, and courage. I also know now that you don't need a whole herd of friends on Earth. But it's OK to have more than one, and it's not necessarily a good idea to put all your eggs in one bucket.' She looked Martha in the eye, her own eyes shimmering and glinting with meaning. 'This is a lovely gift, Martha,' she said. 'But I'm afraid I'm going to have to ask you for something else as well.'

'What?' said Martha.

'I want you to give me some Tips and Pointers, so that I get the Human Handybook right this time. Do you think you could do that for me?'

Martha shrugged happily. 'Of course I will,' she said. 'I'd love to!'

'Goody gum-pops!' said Opal, taking Martha's hand. 'I hope you have a very good time at Jessie's birthday, Martha. And I hope you'll agree to come on that special trip with me some other day.'

Martha was very relieved to hear that the trip wouldn't have to be cancelled altogether because of her. 'I will,' she said. 'I promise. How about next Saturday?'

Opal twirled Martha round by the hand. 'It's a done deal,' she said.

'Aw,' said Robbie. 'It's not fair. We're going to fly like a supersonic wind. I can't wait a whole week.'

'Of course you can wait, Cucumber Hero,' Opal said. 'We all can. Anyway, we've got all the time in the world now. Come on, Earthlings,' she cried. 'Time for a group huggle!' A string of shining stars zigzagged out of her eyes, ready to encircle them.

Martha cleared her throat. 'Should you be doing that, Opal?'

Opal looked sheepish and the starry string zigzagged straight back again. 'Good pointer,' she said. 'No more frivolous eye usage. I'm going to take great care of my eyes from now on. I'm turning over some new leaves. Let's have a good old-fashioned Earth toaster instead.' She grabbed her carton of juice and raised it high in the air.

'To new leaves!' she said.

'New leaves!' said Martha and Robbie, raising their juice cartons too.

Opal knocked her carton together with theirs and cried at the top of her voice, 'Fresh new leaves! And about zooming time too!'

A dream comes true

Martha lets the wintry sea air flow over her. Standing on the ridge of steep-sided rock, she braces herself against the breeze. She is still a little dizzy from the journey and from the knowledge that she has just travelled hundreds of miles in a matter of moments.

The Domestipod has settled next to the lighthouse. It looks as though it has always been here, although the three of them only stepped out of it a few minutes ago.

Martha knew exactly what Muckle Flugga would look like, even before she got here. It's a sharp, stony island, grey as a whale. There's no one else on the island. In fact there's nothing much on the island at all. Only the tall white lighthouse, which flashes brightly every few seconds.

Robbie comes clambering up the side of the rock towards her, as Martha knew he would. He has been dipping his feet in the sea and his toes are pink with cold, as she knew they would be.

Opal springs out of the lighthouse door, her eyes fresh and blazing purple, much brighter now than when she

first went in. Martha waits for Opal to whoop and for the pair of puffins to fly up in panic, startled by her voice.

'Yaaahoooo!' whoops Opal. The puffins flap away over her head and perch high up on top of the lighthouse.

With Garnet fluttering and hovering at her shoulder, Opal bounds towards Martha, taking great skipping strides to reach her.

Martha knew Opal would do that. She knows what's coming next too. So does Robbie. They both know because they have seen it before.

Opal seizes their hands in hers and whirls them round to face the sunset.

The sun is lower now. It looks like half a massive orange dropping down behind the sea. As the sun disappears the sky begins to change colour. Threads of pink appear in the blue. Bronze streaks spread out over the pink, as if an artist is splashing new colours over a giant canvas.

The three friends stand together on top of the island. Opal raises their linked hands and Robbie and Martha reach out with their free arms so that they are like paperchain figures, strong and unbreakable ones, stretched out in front of a shimmering sea.

It is perfect.

It is just as Martha dreamed it would be.